Cathy MACPHAIL

UndeRworld

BLOOMSBURY

LONDON BERLIN NEW YORK

Acknowledgements

Special thanks to 7K 2002–2003
All Saints Catholic High, Kirkby, Liverpool

Bloomsbury Publishing, London, Berlin and New York

First published in Great Britain in 2004 by Bloomsbury Publishing Plc
36 Soho Square, London, W1D 3QY

This edition published in 2009

A CIP catalogue record of this book is available from the British Library

ISBN 978 1 4088 0204 5

The paper this book is printed on is certified independently in accordance
with the rules of the FSC. It is ancient-forest friendly.
The printer holds chain of custody.

FSC
Mixed Sources
Product group from well-managed
forests and other controlled sources

Cert no. SGS - COC - 2061
www.fsc.org
© 1996 Forest Stewardship Council

Typeset by Dorchester Typesetting Group Ltd
Printed in Great Britain by Clays Ltd

1 3 5 7 9 10 8 6 4 2

www.bloomsbury.com
www.macphailbooks.com

Underworld

For my son David

Prologue

I watch Therese playing with our grandchildren. She looks as beautiful to me now as she did when we were seventeen. Therese pulled me through the bad times, stood by me, held me when I would wake screaming from the nightmares. People thought it was the war that drove me mad. I let them think that. Only Therese knows the truth.

I have often thought of writing my story, but the memory has always been too terrifying to face. I am an old man now, and it was so long ago. Who would believe me? And do I believe it now myself?

CHAPTER 1

'So, you haven't brought your PE kit again, Fiona?'

Fiona Duncan stood in front of the teacher, her very stance an act of defiance. Tapping her foot impatiently, balancing her bag on her hip. She made an art of looking bored, staring straight ahead, chewing her gum. She shrugged an answer.

Mr Marks looked just as bored. 'This is the third week in a row.'

'Really? I've not been counting myself.' Fiona's voice was full of sarcasm. That was what broke her teacher's temper at last.

'Yes, really! And this time you are in trouble.'

Fiona blew a bubble. 'Think so?'

'Yes, I think so, Fiona.'

Fiona didn't say anything for a moment, then her face creased into a triumphant smile. 'You can't make me do anything, sir.'

She watched her teacher's shoulders slump in defeat. She had won. She knew she had.

'Yes, you're right. I can't. Just promise me one thing, Fiona.'

'Anything, sir.'

'Don't be a teacher. It's a thankless job.'

She turned away from him, laughing. No fear of that, she mumbled, and she barely caught his next muttered words.

'No fear of that indeed. Once a loser, always a loser.'

She almost spun round then. Who was he calling a loser? Just because she thought his beloved PE was boring. Maybe that was his fault. He was a rubbish teacher. Yet, even as she thought it, she knew it wasn't true. The rest of the class, all dressed in their PE kit, thought he was great. Jumping about, eager to start. She'd held the lesson up. They weren't happy about that.

'What am I supposed to do now, sir?'

He looked at her as if he really would like to tell her what to do. She caught the look, understood it.

'Now, now, sir, don't be rude.'

A murmured giggle broke out in the class.

Finally, Mr Marks shook his head. 'Sit on the bench and do nothing. That seems to be the only thing you're good at. I've wasted enough time on you.'

Fiona threw down her bag and flopped on to the bench. It banged against the wall. She knew he'd probably report her, then she'd be disciplined by the head. Somebody would phone her mum. Her mum would rant and rave at her, and then forget it. Same thing every time. But it was better than getting changed into a nerdy pair of shorts and jumping about like somebody mad.

Zonks! Look at the fat lassie. I wish I had her nerve, Fiona thought. She looks as if she's got a sack of potatoes inside those shorts. She would die before she'd wear shorts if she had a bum that size. She was almost ready to laugh when the fat lassie – was her name Angie? – suddenly let out a disgusted yell. She put her hand to her hair and pulled it away in horror, trailing a long string of spittle on her fingers. She was almost crying. 'Who did that?'

Fiona knew even before she looked up to the walkway that ran above the gym exactly who had done that. Who else but Axel O'Rourke?

Fiona was on her feet in an instant. 'See you! You're disgusting, O'Rourke.'

In answer, Axel aimed another spit directly at her and

Fiona leaped back just in time to miss it.

'I'm disgusting? It should be against the law to let anything that size wear shorts.' He pointed at Angie and laughed.

Fiona glanced at Angie. Her round face had gone red. She didn't know where to look. Fiona yelled back at Axel. 'Have you looked in the mirror recently? There's more craters on your face than on the moon.'

Axel almost jumped over the balcony at her. He didn't like anyone referring to his acne. No one ever did. They usually got thumped. 'I'll make you sorry you said that, Duncan.'

Mr Marks roared into the conversation. 'Right, Axel O'Rourke. Headmaster, immediately!'

Axel did a bolt along the walkway. Mr Marks yelled after him and then he was running out of the gym to catch him.

Fiona looked at Angie. The fat girl's eyes were filled with tears. She was new to this school. If she was going to survive here she would have to learn how to be insulted and to answer back.

'Don't cry over him, honey,' Fiona said, putting her arm around Angie's shoulder. 'He's trash. Ugly pig like him calling you fat. At least you can go on a diet. Him?

It would take more than plastic surgery to make him good-looking. It would take a miracle.' She smiled, but Angie didn't smile back. She wasn't too sure whether she'd just been insulted again. 'Come on, we'll get that muck out of your hair.'

Mr Marks couldn't catch Axel. Even he couldn't run that fast, PE teacher or not. Axel would get it later, but that was later, not now. His mate Liam stood at the door of the school cafeteria.

'What's the rush?' he asked.

Axel looked behind him. No sign of any panting Mr Marks. He flung his bag on a table. 'See that Fiona Duncan, I'm going to get her.'

'Come on, Axel. Even you can't tank a girl. Especially Fiona. She's all right. She's one of us.'

Fiona rebelled. Fiona didn't toe the line. Fiona was always in trouble. One of us.

Axel sat back, still angry with her. She had spoiled the moment, spitting on the fat girl. Fiona had a habit of doing that. Spoiling things. One day he was going to make her really sorry. He was going to say the right thing at the right time, just like Fiona. He was going to make her cringe. She was always too clever with that

mouth of hers. And if he couldn't say the right thing …
then he'd put her windows in instead.

He didn't like Fiona, but not half as much as he
didn't like the two boys who rushed into the cafeteria
now.

The little darlings of the teaching staff. They never
did anything wrong. Now, if he could find a way to get
them, Axel O'Rourke would be one happy boy. He
caught one of those boys glancing over in his direction.
Rick Glancy, blond, good-looking, fancied by half the
girls in the school. His hair colour was natural, not dyed
yellow like Axel's. His skin was smooth. No wonder
Axel hated him.

'What are you looking at, Glancy!' he yelled.

He imagined him answering him back, giving Axel
an excuse to thump him – but he didn't. His mate
Zeshan held him back. 'Don't rise to his bait, Rick,' he
said. 'Ignore him. He can't stand that.'

With a smirk they both did just that. Turning their
backs on Axel as if he wasn't there. As if he was nothing.

One day, Axel thought, I'm going to make them
sorry. I'm going to make them all sorry.

CHAPTER 2

'Zesh and Rick, they really think they are something, don't they?' Liam edged closer to Axel.

Axel didn't answer him. His eyes were still following the Asian boy and his ice-cool blond companion as they sauntered out of the cafeteria.

'I don't know why you let them bother you, big guy. You move in different worlds.'

Suddenly, Axel turned on Liam with such venom that he almost leaped back on his seat. 'They don't bother me at the moment. You and your brown nosing, that's what bothers me at the moment. Where have you been anyway?'

Liam grinned. He had no intention of telling Axel where he'd been. He glanced, for a fearful second, at the entrance to the boys' toilets, expecting any minute for Tony Manza to emerge. Wondering if Manza realised it had been Liam who had chucked the bowl of water into his cubicle. He probably didn't. No one ever suspected Liam. Liam was funny. Liam was a hanger-on. But Liam wouldn't have the guts to confront anyone.

Not to your face anyway, Tony boy, Liam thought, remembering how Tony had humiliated him in the playground earlier. Pulling his jumper over his head, pushing him inside one of the wheelie bins. Liam had pretended it had been so funny. He'd made a joke of it.

But it wasn't funny.

Suddenly, Tony did explode out of the door, swearing loudly. 'Who did that!' he was yelling, and he was dripping wet.

Axel looked up, laughed so much at the soaking Tony, that soon everyone joined in. Casually, Liam looked over. He smiled. Tony's angry eyes darted everywhere searching for a culprit, didn't even look his way. Liam turned away, uninterested now. He was satisfied. No one ever messed with Liam and got away with it.

'What on earth makes Liam and Axel friends, do you think?' Zesh asked Rick as they leaned over the walkway watching what was happening in the cafeteria below. 'They've got nothing in common.'

Rick glanced at Zesh. 'They could say that about us.'

Zesh shrugged. 'My parents are Pakistani, yours are originally Danish. We're both British. I would say we've got a lot in common.'

There was certainly a touch of the Viking about Rick, something noted by lots of the girls in their year.

'I think we're a good match.' Zesh said it with assurance, but then he said everything with assurance. Don't argue. I'm always right. It was the one thing that annoyed Rick about his friend and Zesh knew it. He knew it got everybody's back up, but he didn't care. He was his father's son and his father had always taught him to know what you want out of life and go out and get it.

Zesh turned his eyes back to Axel and Liam. They had started throwing chips and food at each other, at other people. 'But Axel's a thug,' he went on. 'There's no other word for him. Liam could be OK, if he ever thought for himself that is. I just don't understand –'

Rick interrupted him. 'Safety in numbers. Safety for somebody like Liam. Who'll go for him when he's with Axel O'Rourke?'

They watched as Axel picked up a pie and squashed it into Liam's face. He was laughing. So was Liam. So were most of the pupils watching.

But not Zesh. He only turned to Rick and said, 'And who protects Liam from Axel?'

Mr Marks grabbed the pie from Axel's hands, and threw it on the table. He glared at Liam in disgust. 'Is this what you call a friend? Making a fool of you in front of the whole school?'

Liam wiped the pie from his face. He could feel himself go red. He looked around, and sure enough everyone in the cafeteria was having a good laugh at him. He was angry at himself for allowing it, but angrier still at the teacher. Why was he the one getting into trouble? Why not Axel?

'Do you enjoy being a wimp, Liam? Have you ever wondered what it would be like to have somebody actually admire you?'

Liam wanted to yell at his teacher to shut up. But he couldn't find his voice.

The teacher turned from him in disgust. 'Get yourself cleaned up. Or don't bother. There's probably somebody else wants to stick a pie in your face anyway.'

Mr Marks turned his attention to Axel. He grabbed him by the collar. 'You'll be sorry, boy.'

Axel tried to struggle free. 'No, you're the one who'll

be sorry, sir. I'll no' forget this.'

Liam was shaking with anger as Marks dragged Axel off to see the headmaster. People around were still sniggering at him.

He had no intention of forgetting this either.

Liam never forgot anything.

Zesh and Rick walked home together, laughing about the school trip that was planned to one of the wild islands off the west coast of Scotland. Mr Marks would be in charge and both boys were looking forward to it.

'If we get picked,' Rick reminded him. 'They did warn us the numbers were limited.'

'If we get picked? Are you joking? We'll get. No problem about that. It'll be great to get away from this place. This school, some of the scum here.'

Rick gave him a punch. 'Honest, Zesh, sometimes you talk like such a snob.'

'I am a snob. I admit it.'

'And don't we all know it,' someone drawled from a doorway as they passed. It was the unmistakable voice of Fiona Duncan, trying to light a cigarette. 'You two really think you are something. Know what I think? You act like that because deep down you've got an

19

inferiority complex. I read about it in a magazine.' She spat out her chewing gum and held out her cigarette. 'Any of you two got a light?'

Zesh shook his head. 'No, we don't have a light, and we don't approve of smoking.'

'Oh, I might have known. Friends of the Earth here don't approve.'

'You'll end up with lines on your face, black teeth and a deadly disease. Do you know that?'

Fiona laughed loudly. 'So will you, Zesh pal. It's called old age. But I intend to enjoy myself till that time comes. OK? You two are so boring. You never do anything wrong.'

'You make up for us.'

'Somebody has to,' she called after them as they hurried off.

She put the cigarette back in the packet. She didn't want to go home. Didn't want to face the music. Mr Marks would have contacted her mum by now. She would have to handle the overreaction, the screaming, the shouting, the threats ... at least till her mum's favourite soap came on.

But, look on the bright side, at least she would get a light off her mother.

CHAPTER 3

Axel shuffled into the school next morning. This wasn't where he wanted to be – in fact, he'd prefer to be anywhere but here. He swung his bag and aimed it at Liam's head. Liam ducked just in time. He swung round and grinned. 'How are you, big guy?'

'Sick,' Axel said. 'Sick of this dump. Hey, here comes the fat bird.'

Angie saw them, looked around for an escape, but there was nowhere else to go. Axel spread himself in front of her like Jabba the Hutt and barred her way. 'You give whales a bad name, know that?' he said, ignoring her blush.

She tried to sidestep him but he moved to stop her.

'Oh come on, Angie, I just want to chew the fat with you.' He glanced at Liam and laughed. 'And there's sure a lot of fat on you to chew.'

'I'll tell on you,' Angie said, her voice trembling.

That made Axel laugh even louder. 'Oh, I am so scared. Hear that, Liam? The fat bird's going to tell on me.'

Liam didn't say anything. He grinned back, but he looked uncomfortable. Axel darted to the side to stop Angie trying to pass him. She looked scared now. Her puffy cheeks were red and there was sweat breaking out on her upper lip.

'Just let me go,' she said.

'Just let me go . . .' Axel mimicked her voice, tremor and all.

Suddenly, there was another voice behind him.

'Let her pass.'

Axel spun round. Zesh stood there, his face grim. Angie smiled at him gratefully, then she was past Axel and bouncing off down the corridor.

'Oh look, it's the knight in shining armour – well, in spotless school uniform anyway.'

'Why are you always such a moron, O'Rourke?'

Axel stood straight. 'What did you call me?'

'You heard,' Zesh said. He didn't want a confrontation. He had done what he set out to do, help the new girl. He was a prefect, and anyway, no one else was going to do it. Now, he just wanted to move on to his class.

Axel was having none of that. He stood in front of Zesh, defiant, challenging. The last thing Zesh wanted was a fight. He didn't fight, not ever.

He made a move to step away from Axel, didn't see him swing his bag and bring it down on his head. Zesh's legs buckled under him. Axel didn't give him a second to recover. He threw himself on top of him and Zesh went down. Axel grabbed his hair and pulled his head back so roughly that Zesh let out a cry. Axel was ready to squash his face on the floor. Zesh struggled, managed to grab Axel's hand and bit his fingers into his flesh. Axel relaxed his grip, just enough for Zesh to squirm free and turn himself round, bringing his fist up and into Axel's face.

Liam was trying to step back, wanting none of this. A crowd was gathering, cheering them on. Some for one, some for the other. In spite of Axel's reputation hardly anyone wanted to see Zesh win. Zesh won at everything. Always. Saw it as his right.

The two boys rolled together along the corridor. Their grunts were the only sound they made. It was the others cheering that alerted the teacher. Mr Marks suddenly burst round the corner. So angry his eyes were wide. 'Stop this! Stop this right now!'

The crowd scattered. Liam stepped quietly into the boys' toilet, unnoticed. The two boys, still locked together, ignored the teacher. He dragged them to their feet by the collar.

'I will not put up with this. Both of you are on a reprimand.'

He let Zesh go, but kept a firm hold of Axel's shirt. Zesh looked pale and his voice was husky and breathless. 'That's not fair, sir. He started it.'

Mr Marks screamed at him, his anger taking Zesh by surprise. 'I'm not interested in what's fair. There will be no fighting in this school.'

Axel struggled to be free of his grip but Mr Marks wouldn't let him go. 'Think you're smart, don't you, O'Rourke. Told me I'd be sorry, didn't you. You didn't waste any time.'

Axel wasn't listening. 'Let me go!' he yelled, but Mr Marks held firm.

'You're not getting away with this, O'Rourke.' He looked at Zesh, saw for the first time the real pallor in his face. 'What's wrong with you, Zesh?'

Zesh shook his head. 'Not used to fighting, sir.' He was breathing hard. 'Can I go to the toilet, sir?'

Mr Marks hesitated. Then he nodded. 'Back here in

five minutes. You're both going to the headmaster.' He glared at Axel. 'Maybe you should just move into his office, O'Rourke, you spend so much time there.'

Zesh stumbled into the toilet, pushed the door closed. He checked out the cubicles one by one, looking under the doors to see if there were any feet visible.

Thankfully, there was no one there. He fell against the sink, his breath coming in wheezing gasps. With every second it was getting harder for him to breathe. He searched frantically through his pockets for his inhaler, desperate to find it. He never left home without it, his mother would never let him. Just in case. He needed it so seldom now, but he wasn't used to fighting. In his panic he was sure it wasn't there today. He didn't want anyone to know about his asthma. Rick was the only one who knew. Where was it!

Suddenly, he felt it in his pocket, grabbed for it, pulled it out so sharply that it slipped from his grasp, hit the tiles and rolled into one of the cubicles. Zesh let out a moan, got down on his knees. He wanted to breathe so badly he was almost ready to cry. Where had it gone? He saw it had come to rest, hitting against the bowl. Normally, Zesh wouldn't touch anything from the floor of these toilets, but he was desperate. That inhaler was life.

He crawled across the floor, lay flat, too breathless to stand, and stretched his arm under the door for the inhaler. He gripped it as if he was afraid it would suddenly leap from his fingers. He sat up, leaning against the door, and puffed it into his mouth. He breathed deeply, as deeply as he could. Waited a moment, then breathed again. Immediately, he felt his lungs open up. It was like some miracle. He took in the air gratefully. It always seemed to him like a miracle. From no breath, to life, and just because of this little piece of plastic. He breathed again deeply, and then got to his feet. Now he was ready to face anything.

Just in time. Mr Marks pushed open the door as Zesh slipped the inhaler back into his pocket. 'Ready, Zesh?' he asked.

Zesh splashed his face with water. 'Ready, sir,' he answered and he followed the teacher out the door.

There was quiet in the boys' toilets, but only for a moment. Only until one of the cubicle doors opened, and Liam jumped to the ground. He was sure he must be sussed when the inhaler had rolled into the cubicle he was in, but it was only Zesh's arm that had appeared, snatching desperately, and he hadn't even noticed Liam perched on the seat like a vulture.

Liam liked knowing things about people. Things no one else did.

And now he knew Mr Perfect Zesh had a weakness. He had asthma.

CHAPTER 4

'Let me go!' Axel was still struggling wildly as he was dragged up the long corridor to the headmaster's office. Mr Marks was saying nothing, but his face was grim. Zesh had to quicken his pace to keep up with him, and even he was wondering about the anger on the teacher's face. Just because he'd caught them fighting?

'You're hurting me!' Axel made one more futile attempt to free himself. 'I could have you for this.'

'Report me then.' Mr Mark's voice was flat and harsh. When he reached the headmaster's door he almost threw Axel inside.

'What's your problem?' Axel began pulling his jumper back into shape and was taken aback by the vehemence of the teacher's anwer to that.

'What's *my* problem?' He exploded. 'Where were you last night, O'Rourke?'

'None of your business … *sir*,' he added sarcastically.

Mr Marks just stared at him. 'Oh, I think it's completely my business. You'd better have an alibi for last night, boy.'

I might as well not be here, Zesh thought. It's as if they're here on their own. I could sneak out and not be missed. He wouldn't do that, of course. That wasn't his way. Stand up and face the music, that was his way. He wondered what his father would say if he learned that Zesh had got into trouble. He'd be surprised, and angry too. 'Letting the side down, Zeshan,' he could almost hear him say.

Then, an even more horrifying thought rushed at Zesh. What if this spoiled his chances of being chosen for the school trip?

He was so caught up with his own thoughts he almost missed what Axel was saying, until he finally shouted, 'Somebody slashed your tyres, sir?' His voice was triumphant. 'Good for them!'

Mr Marks glared at him. 'As I say, you'd better have an alibi.'

'You should keep your car in a garage, sir. It would be safer.'

'You obviously know I don't.'

Axel's eyes flashed. 'I know nothing. I'm not getting

the blame for this. I get the blame for everything.'

Mr Marks moved his face so close to Axel's that Zesh thought he was about to head-butt him. Way too close. He could see the anger still in the teacher's face. He was inches – seconds – away from losing it completely, and ruining his whole career.

'I'll not let you squirm your way out of this one.'

Zesh saw Mr Marks's knuckles tighten on the shoulder of Axel's jacket. He could see exactly what the teacher really wanted to do. Lift Axel off the ground. Probably throw him through a window. For a second, Zesh was almost sure he would. He was a powerful man, Mr Marks.

'Sir!' Zesh shouted, wanting to break the tension. 'The headmaster will be in assembly now. He won't be back in the office for ages.'

Axel finally managed to pull away. 'You're a head case. Sir!'

Mr Marks took a step back, just realising what he had almost done. He seemed to shake himself, as if he was coming out of a dream. 'OK, both of you go. For now!' He fastened his eyes once more on Axel. 'But you haven't heard the last of this.'

'Slash his tyres? Did you?' Zesh asked as he and Axel

burst from the office.

'Me? Wish I had thought of it.' Axel jumped and punched his fist in the air. Zesh watched him as he ran off, watched him and wondered. You never knew with Axel.

'Axel? Where did he get a name like that?' someone asked Fiona.

'It's short for axe murderer,' she said without a moment's hesitation. 'That's his chosen weapon of mass destruction. Or it will be when he figures out which end is which.'

She laughed loudly, so did everyone else. They had all been speculating about whether Axel was the culprit. The consensus was that he must be. Guilty until proven guilty. It would be too much of a coincidence that some random vandal had chosen last night to slash Mr Marks's tyres, the same day that Axel had threatened the teacher. No, despite his protests, and they were given with a snigger – almost as if he enjoyed being a suspect – everyone took it for granted that Axel was the guilty one. Fiona wasn't so sure. She couldn't say why. It was a feeling. 'Women's intuition.' Ha! That was a joke. She didn't believe in all that hokum.

They were being herded into the assembly hall, herded being the operative word, Fiona thought grimly. She was almost waiting for one of the teachers to produce a lasso and rope them in.

She caught the fat girl, Angie, staring at her. When their eyes met, Angie beamed a smile. She was remembering how Fiona had stuck up for her in PE, and then helped her wash all that disgusting spittle out of her hair.

Oh, goodness, she thinks we're going to be zonking friends now. Fiona half smiled back, and then turned and pushed her way against the crowd, away from Angie. She could see the girl's disappointment. Didn't care. Come on, she thought, me and Moby Dick? Friends? That would definitely ruin her image.

One of the teachers, Mr Yates, barred her way. 'And where do you think you're going, Duncan?'

'Lavvy, sir.' She said it boldly. After all, he was a man. He wouldn't question a girl going to the toilet.

However, she forgot one thing. He wasn't a man. He was a teacher.

'Assembly, Duncan!' he commanded, pointing her back inside the hall.

She turned reluctantly. And found herself face to

face with Angie.

'Hello Fiona,' she said. 'Did you forget something?'

Fiona didn't have time to comment. Mr Yates pushed them both on, together, as if they were meant to be together: friends.

'Come on, girls, aren't you dying to know who's been picked for the school trip?'

The atmosphere in the hall was tense. Fiona couldn't understand why. Just for names to be announced for some zonking school trip? To a Scottish island of all places! Big wow! It would be freezing there, and boring. Walks in the wild, and camp songs around the fire! Whose idea of a school trip was that?

Her gaze moved along the platform where the teachers had lined up, and came to rest on the PE teacher, Mr Marks. Of course, he was the man who climbed Munros for charity in his spare time. She had thought for a while that a Munro was one of the unruly pupils in the school, until she was told it was a mountain that had to be over a certain number of feet. Too much information, she thought. Who else would think of this as a great idea for a school trip? You would think, however, that he might look happier about his dream coming true. Then she remembered his slashed tyres. It seemed to Fiona as she watched him that he looked really angry now.

'It would be lovely to be picked, wouldn't it?' Angie said, her voice full of enthusiasm. She was shaking her head with excitement and her shiny fair hair moved like something out of a shampoo ad. 'Don't suppose I stand a chance, just being new and everything. But I put my name down anyway. Maybe you'll get picked, Fiona.'

Fiona looked at her as if she was mad. 'Me? On a school trip? Come on, Angie, one of the Famous Five I ain't. I never put my name down for anything. So I'm safe.'

Angie looked disappointed. Zonks! She really does think we're friends.

'Aw, I thought it would have been so much fun. You and I, together, like.' Angie shrugged. 'Oh well, I hope I don't get picked now either.'

Fiona almost screamed. She sent out a silent prayer. Not a thing she did very often. In fact, there was a good chance that God had forgotten who she was.

Please. Let her get picked for one of these trips, she prayed. It's the only way I'm going to get rid of her for a while.

On the platform the headmaster called for quiet. No

one listened to him for a moment. No change there. It took the Maths teacher, who was built like a wrestler, to calm them down. Finally, the headmaster got his chance to speak.

'You all know why we're here. There have been two school trips planned this year. One is going to Paris, a beautiful city of culture and legend.' He went on about the beauties of Paris for about ten minutes. Shut up about Paris, Fiona wanted to shout at him. But he wittered on. Then, he called out the names of the twenty pupils who had been chosen for this trip. There were no surprises. The usual suspects had been picked. The good, well-behaved and favoured pupils in the school.

There were whoops of delight, and moans of disappointment. Fiona hardly listened. She had just noticed that she had a broken nail. And she was dying for a fag.

'I'd love to be going to Paris again,' Angie said. 'I love it.'

'You've been there?' Fiona asked her, though she was hardly interested.

'At my last school. Turned out to be a bit of a disaster right enough.'

'How? What happened?'

But Angie didn't have time to tell her. The

headmaster called them all to attention again. The noise quelled. The shuffling stopped. He began calling out the names of those pupils who had been chosen for the island trip.

'Zeshan Ahmed.' The first name he called out. Fiona's eyes found Zesh, looking pretty pleased with himself, but not surprised. He'd expected to go. Arrogant zonker, she thought. His equally arrogant mate, Rick, patted him on the back. She saw him cross his fingers in an exaggerated gesture, as if he needed to. His name would probably be the next one called out.

But it wasn't. There was a list of names mentioned, and Rick's wasn't one of them.

'Angela Ward.'

Angie jumped in the air, screamed, and came down with such a thud she almost went through the floor. She clung on to Fiona. Fiona tried to disentangle herself but Angie was too excited. 'I'm going. I've been picked. I can't believe it!'

Fiona pulled at the fingers clinging round her neck. 'You're strangling me, Angie.'

'Oh, sorry. I am just so excited.'

Fiona took a step away from her, but Angie followed. Well, at least my prayers have been answered, Fiona thought, impressed by the speed of the response. She would have to pray more often, she decided.

They had almost come to the end of the list, and still Rick's name hadn't been called. Zesh patted him as if to say, 'Any moment now, pal.'

But the next name that was called out made the whole school gasp.

'Axel O'Rourke.'

Even Axel looked surprised. Shocked. He looked around as if there might be another Axel O'Rourke here in the hall. Then his face clouded over.

'Me? No way!'

Fiona couldn't hear him, but she saw the gesture he made. She could read his lips. Her eyes darted back to the platform. Mr Marks was watching him with his jaw set firm, and barely holding in his anger. Now she knew why he had looked so angry. He had known that Axel had been picked, and hadn't liked it one bit. She couldn't blame him. Axel O'Rourke on the school trip? The mind boggled. She was so engrossed in her thoughts and there was still such a murmuring in the hall that she almost didn't hear the next name to be called.

'Fiona Duncan.'

CHAPTER 5

We are being attacked. The submarine shudders with every explosion. I have never been so afraid. I do not like tight places and now I am going to die in a coffin of steel.

We are all running, in every direction. Panic has set in. It is clear that we are going down, and I do not want to die this way. I must escape. At least in the water, I might be able to swim to safety, to land. Any land. I must escape.

* * *

Zesh still hadn't come to terms with Axel's name being called. Some mistake, he thought, someone's idea of a joke. He was going to see someone about it. Protest. It wasn't fair if Axel, of all people in the school, got to go on this trip.

'Fiona Duncan?' It was Rick's incredulous voice, repeating the last name called, which brought Zesh back to what was happening. He looked across the hall to where an astounded Fiona was standing, her

38

mouth open, as shocked as Rick was to hear her name called.

'Fiona Duncan!' she bawled at the top of her voice, pointing at herself dramatically. 'This Fiona Duncan?'

Always over the top, always loud, always in trouble. Why was she getting the chance to go? The idea she was going too appalled him. Another loser picked, Zesh thought, pushing out another, worthier pupil.

'And those are the final choices for the two school trips this year. I know many of you are disappointed – but you will be the first choices for the next trip. You have my word on that. But for those of you who have been chosen, I hope you will appreciate and enjoy this wonderful opportunity to broaden your horizons, to widen your knowledge of the world. Who knows what people you will meet, what adventures you will have. This school trip could change your life.'

Zesh hardly listened to the headmaster. He was looking at Rick. Rick, whose name hadn't been called. Rick, who hadn't been chosen.

'I don't believe it,' Rick gasped.

Zesh pulled at his jacket. 'Neither do I. Come on, we're not letting this go!'

Mr Marks, his face grim – Zesh had never seen him look so grim – was striding towards them. He held out his hands in a gesture of anger. 'Don't even say it, boys. I have fought and argued this decision all morning. I'm afraid I was outvoted.'

'But why, sir?' Zesh couldn't keep the anger out of his voice. 'Axel O'Rourke. He didn't even want to go.'

Mr Marks shook his head. 'I hate to say it, but I gave them the ammunition that lost me the battle.' He laughed bitterly. 'How often have I said, "Take a boy for a day in the mountains, and I will bring you back a man".'

What rot! Zesh thought. Axel O'Rourke? You'd only take him into the mountains to assassinate him and bring back his body. He bet that was what Mr Marks was thinking right this minute too.

'So,' the teacher said, 'I've to make a man of Axel O'Rourke.'

'First you'd have to make a human being of him, sir.'

Mr Marks looked at Zesh as if he wanted to agree with him – but felt already he had said too much. He turned to Rick. 'I really fought for you to go.' He patted him on the back. 'Next time, I promise.'

Rick pulled away from his touch. 'Next time

nothing!' And he hurried from the hall, ignoring Zesh's shout after him.

'We were looking forward to going together, sir. We're best pals. We go everywhere together.'

Mr Marks nodded. 'I know, Zesh.'

There was a sudden commotion from the other side of the hall. Two teachers were trying to control a struggling Axel.

Mr Marks's face clouded over. 'He's obviously over-come with the excitement of being picked,' he said, his voice heavy with sarcasm. Then he turned away from Zesh and hurried over to help the teachers.

Zesh looked around for Rick, but he'd gone. He felt sick inside. He'd been looking forward to this trip so much. Now, he didn't care if he went or not.

Liam watched thoughtfully. Zesh was angry, but held in his anger. Typical. Never let himself go. Not really. Not until this morning with Axel. He hadn't wanted to fight. Come to think of it, it wasn't much of a fight. Axel had had the better of Zesh from the beginning. Maybe now that Liam knew about the inhaler, he could understand why. He came across as a cold fish, did Zesh. Above such things as fear, never scared. Even now, when his best friend had lost a place on the trip, he was still calm, still in control.

Rick wasn't. Liam had been pushed aside as Rick strode from the hall, fuming. He looked ready to cry. Liam could see he was shaking with anger. And had Zesh run after him? No, he had stood with Mr Marks, probably chatting about the trip and how he would be a willing helper to the teacher. Foregone conclusion that he would be in charge. Some friend.

Well, he wouldn't be looking forward to it so much now that Axel was going.

Axel.

Liam hadn't expected that either. He had put his name down for the trip in the hope of getting away from Axel, though he'd hardly thought he would be picked. No one seemed to have noticed his name being called out. Liam, the invisible man.

But he *was* going, and now, so was Axel. Maybe he shouldn't be looking forward to the trip either. If Axel ever found out it was Liam who slashed the tyres, what would he do? What would he say if he knew that Liam had meant for Axel to get the blame? He'd got back at both the teacher and Axel, with that one action. Two birds with one stone. If only they knew just how smart

Liam Corrigan could be, he thought, they wouldn't think he was such a wimp. They would start to sit up and take notice of him.

'If you think I'm going on your crappy school trip you're up a gum tree.' Axel was breathless with fury. On a school trip? He'd run away first. He shook the teachers' hands from his shoulders as he saw Mr Marks striding toward him. This was all his fault. He had probably insisted on his least favourite pupil coming along, just so he could keep his eye on him.

'This is all because of your blinkin' tyres, in't it?' He saw the teacher's eyes flash when he said that.

Mr Marks would get him back for that, and something in Axel's belly froze up. On a school trip, anything could happen with a teacher who didn't like him, who hated him, in fact. And Marks hated him.

Was that cold feeling fear? As Marks came close Axel saw what a big man he was, muscled, with his kung fu and the martial arts he taught out of school. Not a man to be trifled with. Away from school, Axel would be at his mercy. Anything could happen.

'I didn't touch your tyres!' He yelled it so loud he took even himself by surprise.

Marks didn't believe him, ignored that protest, came so close to Axel that without realising it Axel took a step back.

'I didn't want you to come. I fought it. But you're coming, O'Rourke, even though you don't deserve it and won't appreciate it.'

'My mother'll have something to say about this.'

Marks's face spread in a slow smile. 'She already has. Her and her ... partner – they think it's a great idea.'

That was like a slap in the face. The boyfriend had a say in it, and whatever the boyfriend, any of her boyfriends wanted, she agreed to. And it would suit this one to be rid of Axel.

'We can't afford it!' he shouted.

'That's where you're lucky too. People like you ... are getting this trip for nothing. The others have to pay, but the powers that be think you deserve to go so much they're willing to fork out public money to get you there.'

'Don't want charity!' Axel yelled again. 'I won't go!'

'That would suit me,' Marks shrugged. 'That would make my year.' Then he leaned even closer. So close no one could hear what he was saying. 'Just remember, O'Rourke, out there ... you're on my territory, in my control. You'll do what I say ... or else!'

CHAPTER 6

Zesh finally caught up with Rick in the English corridor. 'I've had a word with Mr Marks,' Zesh told him. 'It's all to do with so called "political correctness".' He put the inverted commas in with his fingers. He mimicked a plummy voice. 'We have to give the poor deprived kids a chance, haven't we?'

Rick just looked at him and said nothing. His attitude puzzled Zesh.

'What?' Zesh asked.

Rick only shrugged and swung away from him. 'I don't need you to see Mr Marks for me. I can do my own talking.'

This didn't sound like Rick, his best friend. It sounded as if he was blaming *him*. 'I know you can, Rick. Champion in the debating contest and all that.' He smiled.

Rick didn't smile back. 'Second actually. You were

the champion.'

They had never split hairs about that before. There had been a tie – then a secret vote between the teachers. Zesh had won that ballot, but they had always claimed it to be a double victory for both of them.

'Look, Rick. If you're not going, then I'm not going.' It took a lot for Zesh to say that – but if this was going to cause any friction between him and Rick then he really didn't want to go. And did he want to go now anyway, with Axel O'Rourke on the trip?

Rick's reaction to that wasn't what he was expecting either. He was suddenly angry. 'Don't do me any favours. Don't be the martyr.' Rick did a weedy impression of Zesh's voice. 'If you don't go, I won't go.' He turned away from him again. 'Give me a break.'

Zesh pulled him round to face him. 'Rick, this isn't my fault.'

Rick almost sneered at him. 'Isn't it?'

'Wait a minute, Rick. What do you mean by that?'

Rick drew in a long breath as if he was trying to say something, or trying not to say it. In the end he couldn't stop himself.

'Why do you think you were picked and not me?' He didn't wait for Zesh to answer, barging on, barely controlling his anger, his frustration. 'Think, "political correctness", Zesh.' This time it was Rick who sketched the inverted commas in the air. 'Lucky my name's not Omar, they'd really have had their knickers in a twist trying to decide between us. On second thoughts, we'd probably both have been picked and some other sucker would have been chucked off the list.'

Zesh felt as if he'd been slapped in the face. He had never heard Rick talk like this. They had been friends for as long as he could remember. Their parents were friends. There had never been a word about race or colour between them, and now, suddenly, this.

'Right. If that's the case I'm definitely not going. I don't need this.'

Zesh pushed past Rick and hurried down the corridor. He couldn't believe that was the reason he'd been picked. Rick was just hurt and angry because he wasn't going. But if it was ... then it put a damper on the whole thing, and left a bad taste in Zesh's mouth. He was going to see Mr Marks. He could strike his name off his old list. He most definitely wasn't going now!

Fiona switched off her mobile angrily. She'd been on the phone for the past ten minutes trying to convince her mother that this trip wasn't a good idea and that she didn't want to go.

Her mother wouldn't budge. 'It'll be a great experience,' she'd kept saying. 'Treat it like a holiday.'

A holiday! 'I'd rather have two weeks in Benidorm, thank you very much.'

Her mother had only laughed at that. 'Look, you're getting it for nothing. Just go and pretend you're enjoying it.'

Truth was, her mother was probably glad to get rid of her. 'See you, Fiona, you'll be the death of me.'

Well, this trip is going to be the death of me, Fiona thought. Not a single person going on this trip she had anything in common with. Which meant she was going to be stuck with fat Angie. The idea appalled her. She swung round and bumped right into Zesh, charging down the corridor. 'Watch where you're going!' she snapped.

He snapped right back at her. 'Shut up you. Get out of my way.'

Fiona pretended to be shocked at that. She stumbled against the wall in a mock faint. 'Oh, dear, Sir Lancelot's being rude to a lady. Shock! Horror! Will Camelot ever be the same again?'

'Oh shut up!' he said again.

Now she really was surprised. 'What's wrong with your ugly face? You're going on your wonderful trip. Some of us don't want to go. It'll be a nightmare. The school trip from hell.'

Zesh suddenly stopped and looked right at her. 'Tell me the truth, Fiona, do you think I've only been picked for this trip because I'm Asian?'

Fiona placed a finger against her lips, opened her eyes wide as if she was genuinely thinking about it. 'Let me see. I'm going 'cause I'm a troublemaker. Axel's going because he's a deprived child. Now, what's left …' She paused thoughtfully. 'Oh yes, ethnic minorities.' Then she sneered in his face. 'It's not rocket science trying to figure that out, Zesh.'

She had never seen Zesh Ahmed so angry, but he was absolutely furious now. In fact, he was so angry she thought he might just cry. Unfortunately, he didn't. He just turned from her and began to race off down the corridor as if the devil himself was after him.

'No running in the corridor!' Fiona yelled after him, indicating the notice that stated just that, on the wall. She looked at some of the other pupils as they passed her. 'That boy never does what he's told, does he?'

* * *

Zesh found Mr Marks in the gym. He was tidying equipment away, his shoulders slumped. He looked fed up. He was surprised to see Zesh bursting in the door, but he smiled and greeted him. 'Hi Zesh.'

Zesh stopped abruptly at the other end of the gym. 'Just tell me why, sir?' His voice echoed into the high roof.

Mr Marks stopped what he was doing and looked at him. 'Why ... what, Zesh?'

'Tell me why I was picked and not Rick.'

Mr Marks lifted his shoulders. 'No particular reason. It was one or other of you.'

'So, why wasn't it the other, sir?'

He could see understanding beginning to dawn on the teacher's face. Mr Marks laid down the bats he was holding and began walking towards him. 'What do you think was the reason, Zesh?'

'Was it because my name's Zesh and not Rick? Because my skin's dark and not white like Rick's?'

Already he could see the anger growing in Mr Marks. 'Don't you dare start talking like that. You've never come across anything like that in this school, or from the teachers here. Or even from many of the pupils. I know we can't stop racism entirely, we'll always have the Axel O'Rourkes to deal with – but you and Rick have never had that. Come on, Zesh, this isn't like you.'

Zesh hadn't meant it to sound like that. 'This is something different, sir. What is it they call it? Positive discrimination. Well, I don't want your positive dis-crimination, sir. I'm refusing to go. Rick can go in my place.'

'And do you really think Rick would go now, under those circumstances? And do you really think your father would allow you not to go?'

Zesh could picture his father, standing in front of him, holding forth on the good impression he must always give. Just once, he would love his father to stand behind him, stand up for him no matter what. Like now.

'See, right at this moment, Zesh,' Mr Marks went on, 'I don't want to go. I'm willing to cancel the whole trip. But you see, I don't have an option, and frankly, neither do you!'

Zesh turned from him and burst out of the gym as angrily as he had entered it. 'This trip is going to be hell!' he shouted.

Mr Marks went back to tidying away the equipment.

He did it slowly until he lifted one of the netballs and hurled it against the wall.

Liam had watched it all from the walkway, watched and took it all in. He slipped out of view. He didn't want to go on this trip either. Was it really going to be hell?

CHAPTER 7

'Fiona! Fiona!'

'Aw naw!' Fiona looked for a bolthole she could dart through to get away from fat Angie. No chance. Fat Angie was lumbering towards her like a charging rhinoceros.

She was dragging two people behind her, her parents obviously. Her mother was an even fatter version of Angie. She stopped breathlessly in front of Fiona. 'I am so excited, Fiona. This is going to be so brilliant.' She linked her arms in both her parents' arms. 'This is my mum and dad.'

Surprise, surprise, thought Fiona.

Angie's mother nodded warily, not too sure what to make of Fiona. Maybe it was the purple hair. She'd only done it last night and she thought it had turned out rather well. Unfortunately, she seemed to be the only one. However, at least it was different, and she liked to be different.

'Your hair looks great!' Angie said loyally.

Her mum and dad notably said nothing.

'This is my friend, Fiona,' Angie said, gazing at her as if she was the best thing since sliced wholemeal bread.

Fiona felt like curling up in a ball. She began to chew her gum faster, thinking that if she didn't do something quickly she was going to be stuck with Angie this whole trip. And the trip was nightmare enough in itself.

'Oh aye, don't worry about wee Angie. I'll make sure she's all right. I'll never leave her side, you betya!'

At that, she inadvertently dropped her cigarette pack. It landed at Angie's mother's chubby feet.

Fiona let out a startled gasp. (I really should try out for the drama club, she thought.) 'That's not mine. Honest. I was carrying it for somebody else.'

It came out exactly the way she wanted it to. Like a lie.

Mrs Ward's eyes flickered nervously. She looked around for a teacher. She gripped Angie by the shoulder. 'Come on, dear. I want to have a word with Mr Marks before you go.'

Angie managed a little wave as she was being hauled

off. A 'See you later' kind of wave.

I don't think! Fiona decided confidently. With any luck, wee Angie would be forbidden even to talk to the purple-haired, cigarette-smoking bad influence Fiona intended to be.

Zesh looked around for Rick, hoping he might just come to see him off. They had hardly spent any time together since that day. The words spoken had driven a wedge between them. And all because of this stupid school trip. He had lost all appetite for going now. Would rather have cancelled. But Mr Marks had been right, his father would have none of it. 'Rick will come around,' he had said. 'He is a good friend. And you will enjoy this trip, Zesh. It will be good for you.'

His mother, however, had agreed with her son. He should cancel on principle. But who ever listened to his mother? Certainly not Zesh or his father.

He looked around for anyone he might have something in common with. However the others who had been chosen for this trip were not in his year – they were either younger or older, and he knew none of them. They were all milling around the bus, pushing rucksacks and luggage into the hold.

He noticed Fiona Duncan. Holy Moly! What had she done to her hair? Had somebody told her that was attractive? And why was her jaw always going ninety to the dozen with that chewing gum of hers? Her mouth constantly looked like a cement mixer on full speed.

And there was Angie Ward. She looked as if she was getting a lecture from her mum. About what, he wondered? What did Angie ever do wrong? Except eat too much.

Liam was there too, shuffling his feet, trying to pull away from his mother as she fussed around him. Liam would be happy enough, Zesh thought, his best friend was going. If Axel could be called anyone's best friend.

That made him think about Axel. He looked around for him. He hadn't arrived yet. Maybe, Zesh began to hope, Axel wasn't coming. And at the last moment, Rick would be asked to take his place.

If only he had thought to arrange some kind of accident for Axel. A couple of broken legs, nothing major. But it was too late for that now.

Zesh could only wonder what was keeping him.

'I am no' going!' Axel yelled it out like a scream.

His mother was shaking with anger at him. 'What

are you doin' this for?'

'Aye!' her boyfriend yelled back at him. 'You're driving your mother potty.'

Axel knew it was no good. His mother would never stick up for him. She never did. He'd pleaded with her not to send him on this stupid trip – and pleading was a hard thing for Axel to do. 'What am I doing what for?' he yelled again.

'You're always causing trouble,' his mother shouted back at him. 'I'm never away from that school. I'm sick of it. You're getting this trip for nothing. So shut up and go!'

'You only want rid of me so you can be wi' your boyfriend for a couple of weeks.'

'That's just a bonus,' her new boyfriend, Allan, said. He stood blocking the doorway, looking threatening. 'Now, get your stuff. You're going and that's final.'

Axel looked at his mother. 'Just for once, are you going to do something without letting your boyfriend decide it first?'

His mother's hands pulled at her hair in a dramatic gesture. It was all too much for her, it seemed to say. 'See you, Axel, you're giving me a sore headache. How can you no' look on this as a holiday?'

Axel grabbed his bag, and pushed his way past Allan, he with a triumphant grin on his face. He'd won, again. They always did. When it came to Axel or his mother's boyfriend – any of her boyfriends – the boyfriend always won.

The bus was almost ready to go, the engine purring as the last of the cases were stuffed into the hold. Parents and children were saying final farewells. Liam was already in his seat. Axel hadn't come. Liam was almost breathing a sigh of relief and he bet that most of the others on the bus were too. He leaned back in his seat and closed his eyes. Two weeks, and no Axel, no Tony threatening him. Zesh might insult him and patronise him, but he did that to everyone. He thought he was better than everybody else. Maybe Liam would try to be friends with him this trip – after all, he wouldn't have Rick and who else would be there for him to pal up with?

Fiona? Hardly likely. She was far too common for the likes of Zesh.

The fat girl? No, somehow, he didn't think she was quite the kind Zesh would want to spend time with.

Thinking about it, there was only Liam. He might

surprise Zesh. Now that there was no Axel in the picture, and that was what he had hoped for, no Axel, Liam felt free. He stretched himself out, his legs under the seat. And he opened his eyes for one last look. His mum and dad and his two brothers were standing by the car, waving. He waved back. There were Zesh's parents too. His dad looked as arrogant as Zesh himself. Standing erect, he only nodded at Zesh, but his mother kissed her fingers and placed them tenderly against the window of the bus. Zesh looked embarrassed by the gesture. The redhead with the big boobs could only be Fiona's mother. She was as loud as her daughter. Jumping up and down and jiggling all over the place. 'Cheerio, hen. Don't do anything I wouldn't do!'

Fiona peeked over the bag she held over her face. 'Would she no' give anybody a red face? She's a total embarrassment!'

Considering Fiona had purple hair, Liam thought she had a bit of a cheek saying that.

And the fat woman, well, she just had to be Angie's mum. She looked so much like her. She was standing beside Angie's dad, holding his hand. Her expression was full of concern. No wonder. Their daughter was sitting beside the dreadful Fiona.

Mr Marks jumped on the bus. 'Right, is everybody here?'

He looked relieved that the 'everybody' didn't include Axel. He checked his watch. 'I think we've waited long enough for Axel O'Rourke. Let's get this show on the road then.'

Yeah, Liam was thinking, fast, before Axel does turn up.

There was a cheer as the door folded shut. The waving grew frantic, as if the parents thought their children were off to the wars and not on a school trip.

The bus had just begun to move off when a car roared into view. Allan's car. Liam recognised it. Allan was Axel's mother's latest boyfriend. His heart sank. The car drew to a halt and Axel was bundled out. He didn't want to go either. You could see that in his face. Mr Marks spotted him. For a moment it looked as if he wouldn't stop the bus. He did, but very reluctantly. There was an ominous sigh from everyone.

The door slid open and Axel jumped on. His face broke into a sarcastic smile. 'Breathe easy, folks, I'm here.'

CHAPTER 8

I saw death that day, so much death. The bodies of my comrades floating in the sea beside me, the smell of charred flesh. Part of me wanted to give up and let death take me too, but I fought on, swimming against the tide in the ice-cold water, heading towards a gloomy shore. If I could reach the land, I would be safe.

Safe?

It would perhaps have been better had I died in the water.

* * *

'It looks like a prisoner of war camp to me.' Fiona threw her rucksack down in disgust. 'I was expecting a five-star hotel at least.'

She glared at the low corrugated-iron building that hugged the compound. The windows were open and bright yellow curtains fluttered in the breeze. There were flowers blooming along the borders, but there was no disguising the fact – it was a corrugated-iron building.

It was bad enough most of them had been sick on the boat coming over, but to arrive finally at this!

'It's been here for years, Fiona.' Mr Marks lifted her rucksack and pushed it back into her arms. 'But it's been all modernised inside. Twin-bedded rooms for the girls, and four-bedded rooms for the boys.'

Liam shouted out, 'That's sex discrimination, sir.'

Mr Marks didn't even bother to disagree with him. 'I know. It is. Now, come on.'

Angie came running up beside him. 'Does that mean me and Fiona can share, sir?'

Fiona tripped up at that point. Almost fell flat on her face with the shock. Share – with fat Angie. Now this trip really was turning into a disaster.

'Are you sure that's what you want, Angie?' Mr Marks asked.

Are you sure that's what *you* want, Angie? Hey, Mr Marks, how about asking me? Fiona wanted to shout out. She remembered Angie's parents, the worried looks on their faces when the bus was driving off. She'd made such a bad impression … deliberately.

'Sure your mum and dad won't mind?' she said. And she knew by the flash in Angie's eyes that they would. She had been warned against Fiona. Now, why didn't girls like Angie listen to their parents? They knew best. Didn't she understand that? Fiona was a bad influence, or at least she intended to be.

'You're my best friend, Fiona.'

Another shock. What made her think I was any friend at all, Fiona asked herself. She glanced at her teacher and noticed a tiny smirk on his face.

'Well, of course you two girls can share.' He said it with some satisfaction.

Angie jumped in glee, clapped her hands together. 'It'll be great. Just like the Chalet School girls.'

Fiona curled her lip. 'Just like the what?'

'The Chalet School. My mum's favourite books. They're great. Come on, I'm dying to see our room, Fiona.'

As they stepped into the building Fiona gave Mr Marks one of her coldest stares.

A big moose of a woman lumbered towards them. She had lots of black hair, even on her face, and she was wearing shorts. Big fashion mistake, Fiona thought. She was smiling eagerly at them.

'Hello, Mr Marks. Lovely to see you again … and so, this is the latest bunch?'

Mr Marks smiled back and shook her hand. 'This is

Miss Lawton, girls. Any problems you can go to her.'

Fiona decided to get her own back on him. 'Ah, so this is why you were so eager to get here, sir. Wee romance going on is there?'

Mr Marks actually blushed. 'Enough, Fiona, you can get detention even here.'

Fiona whisked out an imaginary notebook and began jotting down on it.

'What are you doing?' Liam asked her.

'Just keeping a list of everything that happens here. Then I'm taking it to the European Court of Human Rights.'

Liam laughed at her. 'First you've got to be human.'

Miss Lawton slapped Fiona on the back and almost flattened her. The woman bellowed with laughter. It was the only way to describe the loud guffaw that came from her. Fiona hoped she wasn't going to be this cheerful for the whole two weeks.

'They've all tried that one, haven't they, Mr Marks? And we always answer, "We're just good friends".'

What a wit, Fiona thought.

Angie was dancing about enthusiastically. 'Can we see our room, Miss Lawton?' She linked her arm in Fiona's. 'Me and Fiona are sharing.'

'Better have a reinforced bed for her. They're not used to elephants sleeping in them.' It was Axel, his rucksack slung over his shoulder.

Angie gasped. A little flush came to her cheek. Fiona threw down her rucksack and rushed at Axel. With both hands she gave him a push that sent him reeling against the wall.

'Well, they better have a rock for you to crawl under, 'cause they're not used to snakes either.'

'You're lucky you're a lassie. I'd thump anybody else for that.'

Fiona urged Axel towards her. 'Come on, big guy. Try it. Think I couldn't take ye?'

Mr Marks jumped between them. 'I don't believe you, Fiona. You're worse than the boys!' He pointed down the corridor. 'Now, get to your room!'

Fiona threw one more defiant dark look at Axel, then she turned and, lifting her rucksack, strode down the corridor. Angie was already by her side, her spirits lifted again because her 'best friend' had stuck up for her once more.

Liam watched them go down the corridor together. One thing about that Fiona, she had plenty of spunk.

But of course, she'd known Axel all her life, lived in the same mean streets that he did. Same kind. His eyes went back to Axel and he was watching them too. Pure malice in that look. He'd get Fiona some way. He'd pick his moment and … Liam shrugged away the thought. It was nothing to do with him.

Mr Marks began allocating rooms for the rest of the group. Boys in one wing of the building, girls in the other. Please, Liam kept praying, don't let me be in with Axel.

But he was. Him and Axel and Zesh, all sharing. Zesh was even more alarmed at the thought than Liam was. So much for his prayers. No one ever listened to them anyway.

'Why have I got to share with him, sir?' Zesh was angry now.

Mr Marks only sighed. 'There is another school coming, and all the rooms have been allocated. And Axel will have to behave himself. I'm in the adjoining room. I'll be keeping a firm watch on everything.'

'This is going to be one awful trip!' Zesh moaned.

'At least we agree about somethin',' Axel said. 'This place is a dump.'

Mr Marks turned on him suddenly. 'Why don't you

ever give things a chance, Axel? This is an opportunity for you. You're not even paying for it. Rick Glancy lost his place just so you could get here. The least you could do is make the most of it.'

'Make the most of this?' Axel sniggered. 'Devil's Island would be better than this.'

'Are you never enthusiastic about anything, Axel? Life is a wonderful gift, can you not see that?'

Axel stared at the teacher as if he was an idiot. 'Life's crap,' he said eventually.

Mr Marks took a step back from him. 'Tell that to somebody who's dying of cancer, Axel. You'll find they would swap places with you anytime. They fight for just one more day of this crap life. And people like you … who've got it all in front of you, are just going to waste it and never appreciate it. Your kind make me sick.'

Axel pushed past him. 'That the sermon finished?' He sounded angry.

Mr Marks was angry too, and it was then that Liam remembered Mr Marks's wife. She had died, just a couple of years ago, and she'd had cancer.

By the time Liam reached their room Axel had naturally picked the best bed, by the window, with a view down into the woods. Birds were chirping outside and there was a strong smell of manure.

Axel slammed down the window. 'That is sick. Cannot be good for you, breathing that in. And if that bird keeps belting that noise out, I'm going to shoot it.' With that he flopped on to the bed and turned his face to the wall.

Liam took the bed as far away from him as possible. At that moment, two weeks away from school didn't sound good at all.

'You always stick up for me, Fiona.' Angie hadn't shut up about it since they'd come into the room. She loved the yellow gingham curtains fluttering at the window and the matching duvets on the beds. And she would keep going on about this zonking Chalet School. Now she was back to her 'new best friend' routine.

'It was nothing to do with you, Angie,' Fiona tried to tell her. Useless. The girl never listened. 'I just don't like Axel O'Rourke.'

'But you always know how to say the right thing at the right time. Do you think you could teach me to do that?'

If I could get a word in, Angie, Fiona thought.

Angie didn't wait for her answer. 'You don't think I'm

too fat, do you?'

Now, this was a tricky one. You looked at Angie and a tub of lard sprang to mind. Couldn't exactly tell her that though, could she?

'My mum says I've just got a slow metabolism.'

Slow? It's come to a halt, Angie.

'I'm a difficult age. When I get older I'll slim right down.'

Like your mother, Angie.

'But while we're here, I'm going to watch what I eat. Exercise. You'll help me, won't you?'

'Oh, you can rely on me.' The sarcasm was lost on Angie.

'I love school trips.'

That was when Fiona remembered something Angie had told her a while ago. 'You said the last school trip you went on was a disaster. What happened?'

Angie flopped on to the bed beside Fiona. The springs made a very funny noise. 'It really wasn't my fault. It was worse than a disaster. It was a tragedy. Somebody got killed.'

CHAPTER 9

Mr Marks seemed to think that a trek in the hills was a joy. There he was, striding out ahead of them, drawing in great lungfuls of air, every now and then turning round to them and calling out, identifying plants and birdcalls for them, trying to get them to appreciate the wonders of nature, the scenery, the hills, the view.

'Listen, that's a willow warbler. Isn't that the sweetest sound you ever heard?'

'Look, a buzzard. They call it a tourist eagle, did you know that?'

'There's a lark. Have you ever seen anything more beautiful?'

'Mmm, and that lovely coconut smell. That's gorse.'

He stopped at the top of the hill looking down over the sea to the magnificent cliffs of the island. 'What do you think of that? The Doon, they call it. There are caves in there, caves that burrow right under this island, a catacomb of caves.'

'Have you been down those caves?' Zesh asked him.

'Wonderful experience,' was his answer.

'Are you not frightened you might get lost in them, sir?' This was Angie, hanging on the teacher's every word.

'Not many people get lost in the caves. The inland caves mostly come out into this magnificent sea cave.'

'Just like doing the toilet. In one end and out the other.'

The teacher turned on Axel. 'Have you always got to be so coarse!'

'You said … not many people, sir.' Zesh took a step closer. 'So, some people have gone in and not come out again?'

Mr Marks didn't answer that one. Instead he turned to Liam. 'Liam,' he said, 'you can draw. Have you ever seen anything like this?'

'Get lost, sir,' Liam called back. Truthfully, he hadn't seen anything quite like this before. The sunlight on the heathered hills seemed to cover them with a purple gauze. And the Doon, with the sea crashing against its rocks. It was breathtaking, but he could never admit that to Mr Marks. Certainly not with Axel watching him. Axel gave him a punch now.

'You can draw?'

Liam shrugged. 'Just stupid stuff. I just do it for a carry on.'

Axel sneered. 'Sure you don't want to be teacher's pet?' He laughed, never a pleasant sound coming from Axel, and then he fell behind the rest of the group.

Liam took the chance to speed up a little, make some distance between them and catch up with Zesh. Zesh was drawing in lungfuls of air too, but with him it looked painful.

'You OK, Zesh?'

He caught Zesh by surprise. He jumped as if he'd just been discovered with his hand in the poor box. 'Fine.' He rasped the word out.

'He's just not fit, wheezing there like an old dosser.' Fiona passed them, still chewing her gum. 'I mean, look at me, fit as a fiddle, told you fags were good for you.'

Zesh managed a smile. Fiona had given him an excuse. 'She's right,' he said. 'Just not fit. Have to get used to these ten-mile hikes again.' Then he moved on, away from Liam, away from them all.

First chance he gets he'll be off somewhere quiet to

use that inhaler, I bet, Liam thought. He couldn't stand Zesh. Why couldn't he admit he had asthma? Was it just because he might not get picked for a team, or wouldn't have qualified for this wonderful wildlife holiday? Or was it, as Liam suspected, because having asthma was a weakness, and people like Zesh didn't like anyone to know they had a weakness?

Well, *he* knew now, didn't he?

There was a sudden shriek from Fiona. 'Hey, did you say a ten-mile hike?' She stumbled up to the teacher. 'Better not be, sir. That's going down in my notebook as well. Against my human rights.'

Mr Marks ignored her. 'Look! Did you see that? It was a chaffinch.'

Axel let out a moan. 'Birdman of Alcatraz, eat your heart out.'

And to his surprise even Zesh laughed.

It was teatime before they got back to the hostel. Angie had loved every minute of the day. She flopped on to her bed and it creaked in agony. 'That was so exhilarating, wasn't it?'

Fiona's feet were killing her and she had blisters. All she wanted to do was stick them in a basin of hot water.

'You know you're deceiving, Angie. You'd think some-body of your size would never be able to walk, and yet here you are bright as a zonking button, driving every-body potty the whole way back with that zonking song you were singing – what was it again?'

Angie beamed, her red cheeks even redder with the exhilaration. 'It's a Girl Guide song.'

Fiona hid her face in her hands and muttered, 'A Girl Guide song. Gimme a break.'

Angie suddenly burst into it again. 'No!' Fiona lifted a pillow and threw it at her. 'Don't sing it again. I couldn't bear it.'

Angie caught the pillow, laughing. She's really enjoy-ing this, Fiona was thinking. Maybe it is something to do with being a zonking Girl Guide. You have to get your brain removed before they let you in.

'You're fitter than that Zesh anyway. He could hardly keep up.'

That had been great to watch, actually. Smart Alec Zesh taking up the rear of the group. It must have been the first time he'd come last in anything.

'Do you think Zesh is good-looking?' Angie asked suddenly, not quite meeting her gaze.

'How? You don't fancy him, do you?'

Angie blushed. So, she did fancy him.

'He stuck up for me. He ended up in a fight with Axel.'

Now, that really surprised Fiona. 'Hey, he fought over you? Maybe it's him that fancies you, Angie.'

That would be something. What a pair they would make.

'Which one do you fancy, Fiona?'

'Is this supposed to be girl talk, Angie? Is this what went on in the Chalet School? Well, forget it. I think they're all a bunch of nerds. All I fancy is a fag. Pass me my rucksack.'

Angie looked troubled. 'You're not supposed to smoke in here, Fiona.'

'You gonny tell on me?'

Angie shook her head. Of course she wouldn't tell. They didn't do things like that in the Chalet School.

'Look, I'll stick my head out of the window if it'll make you happy. No nasty smoke in the room, eh?'

Angie managed a Girl Guide kind of smile. 'I wish you wouldn't smoke, Fiona. It's so bad for your health.'

'Angie hen, sometimes you sound like my mother.' Fiona thought about that for a second. 'No, take that back. My mother shares her fags with me. You're worse than a mother, Angie.'

Angie only looked pleased at that. She didn't seem to realise it was meant as an insult. She began to tidy up the room, lifting the clothes that Fiona had flung around and folding them neatly on a chair. Fiona couldn't get her head out of that window quick enough. This girl wasn't real. She'd read too many books. She thought she was living in one of them. She thought life was a book.

Maybe it was. But certainly not a Chalet School book.

More like a horror story.

Zesh had recovered by the evening meal. He'd been stupid to forget his inhaler in the first place. But once back in the room, he'd sneaked it out of his drawer and it had worked its usual magic. No one had suspected. Axel was too stupid to realise what was wrong with him, and Liam not interested enough. Angie (was she for real with that singing?) was totally oblivious to everything but her surroundings.

Only Fiona seemed suspicious – but she'd put it down to his lack of fitness – and that suited Zesh. Let them think what they liked. For now, he felt great, and it would never happen again. He'd never again forget that inhaler.

'This food is crap!'Axel spat out a mouthful back on to his plate.

Zesh was disgusted. 'Do you do that in your own house …?' He paused. 'Yes, I imagine you do.'

The cook had heard him too. She strode across to them. Her name was Mrs Soames, and she had a face like a horse with constipation. 'I've never had any complaints before,' she snapped. She was waving a ladle about threateningly.

'They probably didn't survive long enough to complain,' Fiona butted in. Mrs Soames turned on her too.

'I can tell you're only used to the best caviare. Chips and peas more like.'

Fiona laughed. 'Aye, but cordon blue chips and peas.' Even Zesh had to smile at that and Mrs Soames saw that too.

'You got a complaint as well? I thought it would be only curries you're used to.'

Zesh's smile disappeared. The woman was nasty. He decided he didn't like her and he was sure she could tell that in his face.

Liam suddenly grabbed at his throat, started to gag. 'Help me, I've been poisoned ... aaaagh ...' and he fell over.

Their whole table erupted in laughter. Mrs Soames wasn't laughing. She lifted Liam by the collar and swung him about. 'Think you're funny, son. A good feed would kill you. You look anorexic.' Liam was trying to struggle free of her but she wouldn't let him go. 'Oh, look at the skinny wee rabbit. He wouldn't even make a good plate of soup.'

Now everyone was laughing, but they were laughing at Liam, and Zesh could see that Liam didn't like it. His face was bright red. Zesh couldn't blame him for being angry. Mrs Soames couldn't make a fool of Axel. He was big and strong and looked likely to thump her without a moment's hesitation. But Liam? He was easy meat for her to humiliate.

Suddenly, Mr Marks was in the canteen, striding towards their table, his face like thunder. 'Mrs Soames. Put that boy down!'

She immediately obliged and dropped Liam, who fell like a plucked chicken to the ground.

Mrs Soames was not the least apologetic. 'You tell them to mind their manners, or they might find something in their meals they're not expecting.' And she slouched back into her kitchen.

'Are you sure she should be working with children?' Fiona asked. 'If you ask me she's escaped from a horror movie.'

'Mrs Soames has been here for years. She's a bit eccentric, that's all.'

'Eccentric? She's a loony!' Fiona snorted.

'I think the food's quite nice,' Angie said, munching.

After the evening meal, Mr Marks and the other teachers who were in charge began calling them all to attention. 'Right, we're going to have a get to know each other game.'

The words had hardly dropped from his lips before Angie was jumping up and down and clapping her hands eagerly. 'Oh, great fun!'

Fiona looked at her as if she was mad.

'You're all going to hang a card around your neck, like this one.' Mr Marks held up a specially prepared white card, with string looped through holes at each side. 'Each of you will be given a pencil and you go around the room and write something about that person on the card.' There was a ripple of sniggers. 'No.

No one is allowed to put anything rude, or detrimental, or negative about anyone. You could say someone has a nice smile, or lovely hair.'

Zesh's glance fell on Axel. What could anyone possibly say that was positive about him? That would be a hard one. Zesh decided he'd just avoid him.

Mr Marks went on, 'No one will know what's written on their back until the end of the evening.'

'I'm not playin' any stupid game!'Axel said.

Mr Marks practically ignored him. 'Game still applies. People can write on your card anyway.'

There were a lot of giggles and laughing as people jostled to collect their cards, slipped them around their necks and began walking around the room looking for who they would pick on first.

It was funny to watch. One really long and lanky boy from the other school was walking about with, 'He's tall, that's about it.'

Someone had written on Fiona's, 'She's a wonderful friend.' It was Angie's handwriting.

And someone else had written, 'She's dead funny.'

Liam's said, 'He can draw.'

Zesh had never known that until today. Why did he hide it?

Mr Marks suddenly rushed up to Angie and began rubbing something out on her card. He glared at a girl from the other school who had smirked as she'd written it.

'Was it something rude, sir?' Angie asked naively.

Zesh had seen exactly what it said: 'She couldn't be much fatter, could she?'

But Mr Marks covered it up beautifully. 'They can't spell "pretty", Angie,' he said.

The girl from the other school sniggered. 'Aye, pretty fat.'

And Fiona stepped forward. 'Aye, but she's got a pretty face ... fat people usually do, and anyway, you're pretty ugly.'

The girl pushed her aside. 'Who are you, the organ grinder's monkey? You're ugly enough.'

Fiona grabbed her by the throat and almost lifted her off her feet. 'You want me to trail you, hen?'

Mr Marks roared with anger. 'That's enough! Fiona, I thought it would be the boys who would be fighting, not you.'

'Oh but Mr Marks, she was sticking up for me.'

Fiona almost went white. 'No, I wasn't. I was sticking up for me! She called me a monkey!' But Angie wouldn't listen. Nothing would stop her from thinking that once again Fiona had taken her side.

At the end of the evening when they read their cards, Zesh's said, 'He sticks up for people.' That was the one he liked best. Had Angie written that? Or had she written, 'He's dead good-looking'? However, he had a feeling it was Fiona who had written, 'He looks too clean for my liking.' Wow! Some compliment.

Angie was over the moon with hers. She hugged it against herself. 'I'll keep this for ever.' 'She's always so positive,' it read. 'That's me,' she said. 'Always positive.'

And Axel? Zesh watched him as he pulled his card off and threw it across the floor angrily. There was nothing written on it. People were probably too frightened to write anything, or were they, like Zesh, unable to find anything good to say about Axel O'Rourke.

CHAPTER 10

Liam waited nearly three days to get his own back on Mrs Soames. It took him that amount of time to come up with his plan. It was a beauty. Just the right thing to make that horrible woman regret what she'd done to him.

He was up early that morning. He had to be. Sneaking out of bed and into the fields. His work done, he climbed back into bed, sure that no one had missed him. So he jumped out of his skin when Axel turned and spoke to him. 'Where were you?'

'Toilet,' he said, and hoped his voice wasn't shaking.

Axel didn't question that. 'I hate this place.' He stared out of the window. 'Food's rubbish, and this is the first day it hasn't rained.' He listened for a moment to the birds singing in the woods. 'And if that dawn chorus doesn't shut up I'm going out there and shooting them.'

Liam was almost tempted to tell him then what he'd done, so they could laugh about it. He decided against it. Liam kept things to himself and that was the best way, he had found. He liked secrets.

'We're halfway through the week, maybe it'll get better.'

'Well, at least it can't get any worse.'

Mrs Soames didn't come in until midmorning. The first thing she always did was to turn on the ovens to heat them for the lunch. Liam had been watching her. He knew her routine. Today every group would be in for lunch, after a morning's woodland walk. No one was going to miss his revenge.

As they neared the hostel, they could hear Mrs Soames screaming at the top of her voice. The smell was horrendous. A smell so disgusting, especially coming from the kitchens, that some people were actually being sick outside.

'What on earth is that!' Mr Marks ran on ahead.

'It smells as if somebody's got diarrhoea and didn't make the lavvy,' Fiona shouted, covering her nose with her sweater. 'I knew her food was bad, but never that bad, surely.'

They all ran, following the teacher, and if anyone

noticed that Liam only strode behind them no one remarked on it.

As soon as they went into the canteen, Mrs Soames caught sight of them and she ran at them. 'You! I know it was you!' She lunged at Axel. 'You did it!'

'Did what? Is that not your stew that's cooking?' He sniffed it. 'Agh, smells good today, Agnes.'

Mrs Soames pushed at Mr Marks. 'See, I knew he had something to do with it.' Her eyes went to Zesh. 'Or him. They're all the same.'

It was easy to see that Zesh was surprised by her outburst at him. He wasn't used to that. But her accusing gaze didn't even touch Liam.

Mr Marks stepped forward. 'Was it you, Axel?' His voice seemed to answer the question. Of course it was Axel. Who else could it have been? And Axel didn't help matters with his answer.

'I just wish I'd thought of it.'

'What happened, anyway?' Liam asked, keeping a straight face.

Mrs Soames jumped forward. She was ready to lift Axel by the throat. Luckily, Liam thought, Mr Marks was there in front of her. And anyway, Axel was built like a horse.

'What happened?' she yelled. 'I'll tell you what happened. Some dirty so-and-so put cow dung in my ovens! Cow dung, and I started heating it up this morning!'

Fiona burst out laughing. Even Zesh laughed. Only Angie looked as if she might cry in sympathy. Their amusement only made Mrs Soames even madder. 'See!' she shouted at the teacher. 'I told you they were a bad lot.'

That only made them worse.

'I don't know what you're laughing at,' she screamed at them. 'It only means there will be no dinner for you tonight!'

Axel almost fell over laughing. 'Every cloud has a silver lining.'

They were all taken to the local chippy that night for their food. It was supposed to be a punishment. It was the best meal they'd had all week. Mr Marks still wasn't happy with them, especially Axel, sure that he was the culprit.

And Axel didn't deny it.

'How do you not tell him it wasn't you?' Fiona asked him more than once.

'Let him think what he wants. I don't care,' was his answer.

That night back at the hostel Mr Marks outlined their itinerary for the next day. Another joyful hike in the wild, finishing with his special treat, 'Though I don't think you deserve it,' he told them. The caves. He was taking them down into the caves.

The caves on the island, he said, were spectacular. Famous throughout the world for their grandeur, some explored and some unexplored. An adventure he felt they couldn't miss, even if they didn't deserve the chance.

'Caves? Underground? He thinks I'm going into some grotty old caves? In his dreams,' Fiona complained.

After the teacher left them, they sat around the coal fire in the communal sitting room, angrily discussing the next day's trip. Fiona was desperate for a cigarette, which was doing nothing to help her mood.

'What is it with him and these caves? How can anybody enjoy being buried alive?' This was Axel.

Fiona turned on him. 'I thought you would understand, Axel. Worms like you are usually found under rocks, are they not? You should feel quite at home.'

There was a gasp from everyone. Fiona held Axel's

stare. For a moment she wasn't sure if she'd gone too far. Had she given him just that one push that would send Axel over the edge? She tried not to swallow, stared him out.

'Bitch,' he said.

Fiona breathed with relief. Axel could never match her in the mouth department.

'Talking of worms ...' The voice of Mrs Soames took them by surprise. She stood in the doorway watching them. The light from the hall was behind her, she was only a silhouette, and the glow from the fire was sending eerie shadows across her face.

'I hope you're not here to tell us any ghost stories,' Fiona said drily.

Angie shot forward in her seat. 'Oh, I love ghost stories. Go on, Mrs Soames, tell us a ghost story.'

She shook her head. 'Oh, I wouldn't dream of telling you young people a ghost story. Not away out here, totally secluded in the dark woods.' She grinned. 'I thought I would tell you a bit of history, instead.'

History, Fiona was thinking. Ghost stories she could handle, but history? Forget it. She got to her feet. 'I'm goin' to my bed.'

Mrs Soames stood in front of her, barring her way

out of the room. 'Uch, sit yourself down. Do you not want to hear the legend?'

Fiona sighed. 'And what legend would that be ... The legend of the cook that cooked dung?' She giggled, and Mrs Soames's face grew dark.

'There's lots of legends about caves. Caves are strange, mysterious places. They're like catacombs under this island, winding everywhere. Lots of stories about them. After Culloden, you know, a lot of the Jacobites hid out in the caves. Some of them never came out.'

Fiona looked around them. 'One of them kind of stories. Somethin' in there, got them, didn't it?' She didn't sound impressed at all.

'Have you never heard of Sawney Bean?' the cook asked. They all looked at her blankly. 'He lived in caves, him and his children and grandchildren. They used to kill, and rob and then ... they would eat their victims. Well-known fact, Sawney Bean and his family of cannibals.'

Angie was loving it. 'Did they live in these caves?'

'No, my dear. Nothing could live in *our* caves ... for long. Even Sawney Bean.' She was being deliberately dramatic, and Fiona was getting annoyed with her. A cigarette, she was sure would put her in a better mood.

'OK, so no cannibals.' Fiona was beginning to get bored again. 'So what have you got?'

'During the Reformation, the priests used to hide in the caves too. And for a time smugglers used them as well.'

'Smugglers?' Liam said, interested. 'Aha! There might be gold in them thar caves.'

'There's something in there guards any gold, let me tell you. Because there were smugglers that never came out either.' There she went with the ominous voice again. She's been watching too many movies, Fiona thought.

'During the war the army started to use the caves for developing secret weapons. But it didn't last. The soldiers got afraid, couldn't stay in the caves for long.'

'This is so interesting,' Fiona drawled. 'Though I think I have enjoyed watching paint dry even more.'

'Shut up,' Zesh said, looking enthralled. Once again Fiona thought that he and Angie were two of a kind.

'During the war a Nazi submarine was torpedoed and some of the sailors survived. They tried to hide out in the caves. Deeper and deeper into the tunnels they went … but only one of them came out …'

'Don't believe this rubbish,' Axel said.

'I suppose when he came out,' Zesh said, laughing, 'he was stark raving mad at what he'd seen?' He pulled at his hair and put on a mad face. In Fiona's opinion it was an improvement.

Mrs Soames didn't even blink. 'He was mad all right. Mad as a hatter. He had seen the Worm … and that's what got his friends.'

'I've seen lots of them,' Axel said.' Used to cut them up and fry them. Didn't do me any harm.'

Angie turned on him. 'Oh, you didn't, Axel. That's cruel.'

Axel ignored her. 'I don't believe a word she says.'

But Zesh was curious. 'Go on, Mrs Soames, what's this about a worm?'

It seemed to Fiona that Mrs Soames's smile changed then, or was it the flickering firelight? Or was she just tired?

'They do say the reason we have all these winding caves is because they were made by the Great Worm, burrowing its way through the earth.'

'Yuch, that is gross.' Angie grimaced at the thought.

'So, this is one of these Loch Ness Monster type of legends.' Fiona was suddenly bored again. She hated

Loch Ness Monster stories. 'I suppose nobody's actually took a picture of your Great Worm either?'

'Plenty of people have seen it,' Mrs Soames said quickly, 'but they're not believed because they never have any proof. We've got no doctored photographs of the Great Worm, you see. But there's people been lost in there, and they've never been found.'

'And you think the people who never came out were eaten by … the Great Worm?'

Mrs Soames didn't actually answer Zesh. Instead she told them yet another story. 'They say its breath is like poison. And its lair is deep in the bowels of the earth. What wakes it up is the scent of a human. And tomorrow there is going to be a lot of humans in those caves.'

Fiona had had enough. 'I don't believe I'm listening to this crap. I mean, at least Loch Ness has got a monster. You've only got a zonking Worm.'

'I think a Worm's scarier, Fiona,' Angie said. Her face was pinched with fear.

'Och, you're a Girl Guide, Angie. You'll probably get an extra badge for fighting it off.'

'We don't have to worry,' Axel sniggered. 'If we meet up with this Worm, we'll throw Angie at it. If she doesn't flatten it, it'll take it a couple of weeks to eat her.'

'If we threw you at it, we could probably poison it,' Fiona snapped back at him. 'Two worms with one stone.'

She was always too quick for him. Before he could think of an answer the moment had passed. But he'd get her for it someday. She could almost see that written all over his face.

'Laugh all you want now,' Mrs Soames said, 'but tomorrow, when you're deep down in those dark caves, and you hear strange noises and smell strange smells, you'll remember about the Legend of the Great Worm, and you'll be afraid then all right.' And she left them, chuckling to herself.

'Is she allowed to do that? Trying to frighten us like that? I'm putting her down on my list.' Fiona was ready to fly after the cook.

'She's only telling us a story,' Zesh said. 'I bet if our school trip was at Loch Ness, we'd be taken out on a boat and someone would try to scare us with stories about Nessie. You're not scared, are you, Fiona?'

That got Fiona's back up. 'No. I am not. But look at poor wee Angie, she's nearly wetting herself.'

Angie almost snapped at her in embarrassment. 'No, I'm not! I think she made it all up. Why have we never heard of this Worm? I mean, at Loch Ness you can buy floppy hats of the Monster. It's a worldwide industry.'

Liam fell back on the floor laughing. 'You want a floppy hat of this Worm?'

The idea seemed to appeal to him.

It appealed to Zesh too. 'Or you could get Worm rock.'

Soon they were all laughing, even Angie.

All except Axel. Fiona noticed that he couldn't even raise a smile. And she wondered if he was afraid.

*　*　*

I thought I was going to die that day. I am still amazed I am alive. Alive when all my comrades perished, all except me. And Captain Goldner. We lie at the mouth of the cave, almost dead with exhaustion. I want to cry. My friends are gone. Our submarine destroyed, and we are here on our enemy's shore. I think of my home in Munich, my mother and my little brothers. She did not want me to leave, but what choice did I have? What choice did any of us have?

For a moment I think the Captain is dead too. No luck there. He turns his face to the sky and breathes in deeply. My mother says the devil looks after his own, and the devil has looked after the Captain. All my comrades, good decent men, are dead, and he who hates the world, is alive.

He turns to me. His eyes are as cold as the sea. 'We seem to be the only survivors, Lothar.'

'Yes, sir,' I say, and I almost salute. The habit of a lifetime dies hard.

He watches me for a while, as the waves surge into the cave. I wonder if the tide is coming in and if, after all this, we are still going to drown.

'We go in the cave,' he says, nodding to the gloomy interior. 'We'll be safe there.'

CHAPTER 11

'Have we got to do this, sir?' Liam wasn't happy. 'I feel stupid.'

They were all kitted out in authentic caving gear. Mr Marks had insisted on it. Wellies, helmets with head-lamps, waterproof suits and first-aid kits. They had ropes attached to their belts, and whistles round their necks. Underneath they were wearing old warm clothes too.

'It's not just for safety reasons,' the teacher explained, 'but I want you to experience the real excitement of caving.'

'The excitement! Wow, about as exciting as trainspotting.' Axel felt stupid too. He was angry he had to wear a helmet, with a lamp attached to it. 'And by the way, I feel stupid as well.'

'You feel stupid! At least you started off looking stupid,' Fiona said. 'But I'm just a young girl – and look at me! I'm like something out of a horror picture.' She did a turn like a model on a catwalk, and plucked at the chin strap on her helmet. 'If my mother could only see me now!'

Mr Marks let out an exasperated sigh. 'You're supposed to look on this as an adventure.'

'I'm looking forward to it, sir.' Zesh, of course, standing straight, actually looking good in the ridiculous gear.

'Me too, sir. I think it's dead exciting.' This was Angie, looking as if she was going to ooze out of the waterproof gear she was wearing.

What was it with that girl? Fiona thought. She was always bouncing like the rubber ball she resembled. She seemed to have gained in confidence too since they came here. Was that because she felt Fiona was her best friend? Actually, Fiona couldn't stand her cheerfulness. They could all see that. Why couldn't Angie?

'Sure it's not that big Worm you're scared of, Liam?'

Liam spun round and faced Axel.

'What's all this about the Worm?' Mr Marks asked.

'Mrs Soames tried to scare us with it last night,' Liam told him.

Mr Marks shook his head. 'It's just a legend. A stupid legend.'

That shocked Liam. He had wanted the teacher to say it was all made up, just to frighten them. That there was no legend of the Worm.

'You mean … it's true, sir?'

'No. It's not true. It's a story. Like the Loch Ness Monster. You don't believe in that, do you?'

Axel answered for him. 'No. But I wouldn't go swimming in Loch Ness, just in case.'

Mr Marks smiled at him. 'Well, Axel. Please don't force yourself to come. I'll get someone to take you back. I believe there's an embroidery class going on this afternoon.'

If only he hadn't said that about the embroidery class. Axel wouldn't have come, Liam could see that. He had been looking for a way out. He had even made a movement to pull off his helmet – until the mention of the embroidery class. There was no way he would go back now.

'We're wasting time!' Axel said, with a glare at the teacher.

Mr Marks held him back. 'Before we go down here, I want to say one thing. In here, we have to work as a team. That's what caving is all about. We're not going in far, just down deep enough to give you a taste of it. But I want you to imagine how it would be.' His voice took on the enthusiasm of a fanatic. 'The thrill of the unknown. The excitement of being somewhere very few people have been before. Of knowing that you might just discover a passage, a chamber never yet found.'

'The thrill of bumping into the Great Worm.' Fiona was laughing. She made them all laugh as they followed the teacher inside the gaping mouth of the caves. Liam laughed too. But he wished with all his heart that he had the courage to say that right now he'd much prefer the embroidery class.

*   *   *

I am so cold. Why am I following this man I loathe, following him into a blackness that seems to be swallowing us up?

'Do you know where you are going, sir?' I ask.

He does not turn to answer me.

'Before the war, I lived on this island. I know it well.'

He stops and shines his torch through the cave. There is nothing to see but rock. Black rock. We are in a coffin of rock.

He says again, 'I know it well.'

'Should we be going in so far, sir? No one will find us.'

At the mouth of the cave we would soon be picked up by the British. We would be fed and given warm, dry clothes. My friend, Dieter, had told me the British do not take prisoners. They would shoot us. I do not believe that. It is propaganda. And now, I am so cold I don't care.

And Dieter is dead and cold now. Cold for ever, under the sea.

'Are you questioning an officer!' He shines his light on my face. I cannot see his. He is only a voice, a voice full of hate.

'No, sir,' I say.

'We go in deeper,' he says, and he turns from me again.

I will not be lost in these caves. I will make sure I find the way out. For I am afraid as I follow after him. There is something sinister about the dark in these caves – as if something is in here, waiting for us.

*   *   *

Funny how silent it was when you were inside, Zesh thought. Not as dark as he'd expected, but this cave was well used not just by cavers, but by tourists too, so the entrance and the railinged stairway leading down to the main chamber were well lit by lamps hanging from the roof. 'Not many tourists here today, sir.' He caught up with the teacher.

Mr Marks nodded. 'We're not in the main tourist

season, Zesh. And we haven't had good weather. But you wait till summer. It's busy then.'

Axel called out to him, 'You mean people actually come here for their holidays?'

The teacher ignored that. He was too pleased with Zesh's enthusiasm.

'It's bigger than I thought, sir,' Zesh said.

'Yes, isn't it? You know, Zesh, sometimes you push through the tiniest space and it takes your breath away to find you're in an underground cavern as big as a football field.'

Zesh was astounded. 'Honest? It really is an exciting world, isn't it?'

Zesh could see the excitement in Mr Marks's face. He was in his element here, wanted to share with them that excitement.

'Now, when we get down, I can show you the passages which lead off from the main chamber. If you keep going down, you'll reach the sea. As I've told you, a lot of the inland caves lead out to the Doon.'

The Doon, Zesh remembered, was the breathtaking cliff on the far side of the island.

Mr Marks went on, 'The other tunnels are roped off for the experienced cavers. So no going off on your own.'

'Could you get lost, sir?' Liam asked him.

'You could always get lost, Liam. That's why you have whistles, so in case you get separated you can find your way back to each other. But head down, towards the sea and the chances are you'll come out. And you leave signs to follow in case you have to come back. Not that we're going very far. This is supposed to be an adventure, not a tragedy.' He turned to Angie as she stumbled on a step. 'Be careful, Angie. Don't want you to fall.'

Axel's laugh rang out through the cave. 'Don't worry about her. She'd bounce.'

Mr Marks swung round at him. 'Did you hear anything I said, boy! You treat every member of your team with respect. Your life might depend on them.'

Axel still couldn't keep his mouth shut. 'Don't think my life'll ever depend on her. And anyway, I don't want to be part of a team.' He punched his chest with pride. 'I'm a loner.'

Fiona chipped in. 'Just got one letter wrong, Axel son. You're a loser, not a loner.'

Axel almost jumped at her, but Fiona stood her ground. 'One day that mouth of yours is going to get you into trouble,' he said.

Mr Marks pulled Axel round and pushed him in front of him. Fiona waited until the teacher was between them before she spoke again. 'I'm shaking in my wellies.'

Angie sidled up to Zesh. 'She's wonderful, isn't she Zesh?' She beamed him a smile. He hadn't realised she was this close to him. 'She always sticks up for me. Just like you. With you two here, I'll be scared of nothing. Even the Great Worm.'

'Shut up about the Worm!' Liam snapped as he brushed past her.

He's afraid, Zesh thought. Doesn't want to admit it but that legend has given him the jitters.

Fiona brushed past them too, smirking. 'On you go, Angie. You and your boyfriend Zesh can take up the rear.'

Angie giggled and Zesh fumed. For once he agreed with Axel. One day, Fiona's mouth was going to get her into trouble.

When they reached the floor of the main chamber the tunnels spread out like tentacles, or – Liam shivered as he realised what they reminded him of – worm holes.

Giant worm holes. He could imagine this Great Worm burrowing its way through its own underground kingdom. He looked at his watch: how long would they have to stay in here? His watch had stopped. Was that something about being underground, or had the battery just worn out? He gazed up the railinged stairway to the entrance. He couldn't see it any more. Couldn't see daylight. And he wanted to see daylight very badly.

It seemed to him that they'd been down here too long. Mr Marks had lectured them on teamwork, on the joys of tunnelling and potholing. But he had also warned them of the dangers, of how quickly caves can flood. He had told them about survival. What cavers do in case of an emergency. How they all work together. Zesh was totally caught up in it. No surprise there. Teacher's favourite, old Zesh. Rick had been forgotten very quickly. He wondered if Zesh and Rick would ever really be friends again. Axel looked bored, sitting on a rock, seeing how far he could spit.

Fiona sat on a rock too, studying her nails and chewing gum furiously. She looked bored stiff too. Angie couldn't decide whether to sit beside her, or stay with Zesh. She couldn't see that neither or them wanted her there. She was fat, and stupid.

'Are we going for something to eat, sir?' Fiona yelled. 'I'm starving. My belly thinks my throat's been cut.'

Her voice echoed through the tunnels and a low rumble could be heard in the distance. She was on her feet in an instant. 'What was that?'

'You shouted too loud, idiot!' Axel yelled back at her, his voice ten times as loud. 'You could cause an avalanche.'

Zesh sniggered. 'I think you'll find that's snow, not rocks.'

Axel just glared at him, then his eyes flashed as another low rumble, closer this time, took them by surprise.

'Time we were heading for the surface,' Mr Marks said calmly. 'And don't worry about the noises. There are always noises in caves. Rock falls in the distance. No danger to us.'

And that's when it happened. It was like an explosion, rocking the ground beneath them. Even Mr Marks looked alarmed. Though his voice was even calmer as he spoke. 'Right, up the path now. Quickly.'

Axel was the first one up there, taking the steps two at a time.

'What was that, sir?' Liam wanted the teacher to say again, distant rock falls, no danger to us. Instead, he shook his head.

'I don't know, Liam. We have had a lot of wet weather, could be that. But these are very safe caves. Well used, we'll find out when we –'

Fiona screamed as the whole cave shook with the next explosion. It was the only way to describe the noise. An explosion. What was happening!

'It's terrorists! They're bombing!' Axel ran up even faster, but the others were only steps behind him. Even Mr Marks was running, pushing the girls ahead of him.

'What's happening, sir?' Zesh's eyes were wide with alarm.

Mr Marks didn't have time to answer him. The next explosion was deafening and so close it only took Liam a moment to realise what it was. Seconds later Axel reached the surface and yelled, 'The opening's blocked!'

CHAPTER 12

Fiona pushed past Axel. 'What do you mean, it's blocked?' She hoped he was lying, trying to scare them. But the entrance had gone, blocked by an avalanche of rocks and boulders.

Mr Marks put a reassuring hand on her shoulder. 'People know we're here. We'll just wait and they'll come and dig us out.'

'When?' Liam asked breathlessly.

'Soon, Liam. I've told them we'll be back no later than six o'clock. If we haven't returned by then they'll know something is wrong.'

'This is your fault!' Axel shouted. He had a vicious look on his face. 'You should never have taken us down here. I'll make sure you get sued.'

'Shut up, Axel.' Zesh came and stood beside the teacher, like his ally. 'You couldn't have foreseen this, could you, sir?'

Mr Marks managed a smile. 'No, Zesh. It should never have happened. This is a tourist cave, that's why there's handrails and a path leading to the lower chamber. I can only imagine the wet weather has caused some kind of landslide.'

A tourist cave? Well used? Fiona wondered. Except this wasn't the tourist season, was it? They hadn't seen a soul on the way up here. The place was deserted. They could be stuck in here for hours yet.

Axel whisked out his mobile phone. 'I'm calling the cops.'

He was bashing the buttons even before Mr Marks told him it wouldn't work underground. 'Especially now that we're cut off.'

Cut off? What was he using those depressing words for? Fiona stepped forward. 'Couldn't we start digging ourselves out sir?'

'Yes, but you have to be very careful. There might be another rockfall.'

Axel sneered at him. 'Good job we've got you here. We might be in trouble if we didn't.'

The situation, the feeling of being cut off, had already made him stop calling the teacher 'sir'.

'It would do you better to come up with some

productive ideas, O'Rourke.'

Axel wagged a finger at him. 'You're going to be sorry.'

Mr Marks turned away from him. 'You make a list too then, Axel, just like Fiona's. I don't really care.'

Suddenly, Axel yelled, 'I'll get us out of here.' And to Fiona's horror he jumped on to a pile of boulders blocking the entrance. He climbed, stumbling to the top and began throwing boulders and rocks wildly in all directions.

'Axel! Come off there!'

Axel wouldn't listen to the teacher. He was panicking, that's what he was doing. Fiona was sure of it. 'Axel, you could cause another landslide,' she shouted.

Zesh started throwing rocks and stones aside as quickly as Axel. 'Or maybe he'll just get us out of here, sir.'

Liam joined him, but still the teacher shouted out to Axel to come down. Axel wouldn't listen.

'Watch where you're chucking your zonking boulders, O'Rourke.' Fiona leaped aside as one of them just missed her. Axel still didn't stop – he didn't care about the rest of them, she knew that. Axel was simply digging himself out. No one else mattered.

Angie picked up one single stone daintily. 'We'll laugh about this later when we're having our dinner back at the hostel.' She said it breathlessly. 'Won't we, sir?' Angie wasn't looking for reassurance. She really believed it. Always look on the bright side of life, right enough, Fiona thought.

Zesh stood straight. 'What's that!'

Fiona heard it too. She strained her ears for calls from the other side of the rock wall. But there was nothing. Yet they all stopped, listened.

Even Axel. 'Don't hear nothing,' he said, but he didn't continue clearing the rocks. He still listened, and Fiona thought it was the very silence that alerted them, an ominous stillness they could all sense.

'Axel, get down from there now.' There was so much quiet force in Mr Marks's voice that Axel jumped to the ground beside him. 'I want you all to make your way back down to the main chamber. Now.'

Fiona followed his eyes. They were looking up at the roof of the cave. Hadn't it been solid stone when they came in? Now, it seemed loose, hanging as if by slender threads of rock.

'Get back to the chamber. Hold tight on to the railing.' Mr Marks was pushing them roughly ahead of him, and Fiona could hear his breath, gasping. 'Go now!'

They began to run, just in time, as the whole cave seemed to explode again, but it was only rock, held together for eons, now breaking free from mother earth. Fiona screamed as the roof literally caved in, and boulders and rocks and stone cascaded down.

Axel was in front bounding down the stairway with Liam and Zesh close behind him. Angie glanced back at Fiona, mouthed to her, 'You all right?' Fiona only pushed her on. She let out a shriek as stones struck her ankles but it didn't slow her. Mr Marks was yelling behind them. 'Run! Run! Run!'

Suddenly, Mr Marks pushed Fiona so roughly she was pitched forwards. She fell against Angie and both of them tumbled forwards. They had to hold tight on to the railing to stop themselves from going over.

But Mr Marks, trying to help them, wasn't holding on at all. He pitched past them and with a wild cry he toppled headlong over the railing, hurtling down to the chamber below.

This was a nightmare. Fiona's thoughts were a scream inside her head as they raced down the stairs. The roar in the cave suddenly stopped and all was silence again. Except for a trickle of stones and rubble settling on the floor of the chamber. They all ran to Mr Marks as he lay, twisted and still. They stood around him in a circle looking down at him. Fiona looked at everybody, one by one.

Liam, she could actually see his heart thumping through his clothes.

Zesh looked pale and scared.

Axel, even now, still managed to look angry.

And Angie, with tears streaming down her chubby cheeks.

Fiona was crying too, trying to hold them back, not managing it. She stared down at the teacher. 'He's dead, isn't he?'

CHAPTER 13

Zesh bent over the limp body of the teacher. 'He's not dead,' he said flatly. 'Just unconscious.'

'But he's badly hurt, isn't he? Must be the way he fell.'

Zesh saw that Liam was shaking, his lips white with fear.

'Do you think he's broken anything?' Fiona looked more sick than scared.

'If not, I'll gladly break something for him!' Axel swung his foot out, ready to kick him.

Zesh sprang to his feet. 'Don't be so stupid. Look, we're in terrible trouble.'

'Thanks to him,' Axel spat at the teacher.

'Somebody will come and get us soon.' Angie looked at Zesh hopefully.

Zesh didn't think that was true, but should he tell her that? Fiona decided for him. 'Don't be daft. Nobody'll get through that rock now. It's blocked solid.'

They all looked up. She was right. A wall of rock blocked the entrance now. It would take dynamite to clear it.

'What are we going to do, Zesh?' Angie was looking at him as if he should know. He wanted to know.

'We'll wait here till Mr Marks comes to. He'll tell us what to do.'

Axel was stamping his feet impatiently. 'And what if he doesn't? What are we going to do then?'

'Look, Axel.' Zesh was just as impatient. 'Maybe it was you caused that second landslide. Throwing boulders all over the place. So just shut up and let me think!'

Axel took a step back. 'Let you think! Do you think I'm going to listen to you?' He looked up at the blocked entrance. 'If there's another one of them explosions that rock'll be coming down here. I'm not just waiting around for it to happen.'

'But where else can we go?' Liam asked him.

Axel's eyes roamed the tunnels leading from this chamber. 'In there, they must lead somewhere.'

Liam was shaking his head. 'I'm not going in there.'

Axel grinned. 'Thinking about the Worm, are ye?' He paled as soon as he had finished speaking. Sorry he had brought it up. Zesh felt it was a memory they had all pushed down deep into their subconscious, away from all their thoughts, till Axel had brought it bubbling to the surface.

Fiona jumped at him. 'That's just a stupid story. Don't even talk about it.'

Axel looked at her as if he wanted to thump her. 'Well, I'm still not staying here. Worm or not.'

Liam tried to persuade him. 'We've got to, Axel. They'll come for us. They will. And we've got Mr Marks to think about as well.'

'I don't care about him.'

Zesh was trying not to get angry. 'If we stay here, at least there's light. They will come for us. Through there …' He pointed up. 'So we stay here.' He said it with confidence, expecting to be obeyed. He was a school prefect after all. He should be in charge now.

Axel took a step away from him. 'You do what you like, pal. I'm going.'

'Going where?' Zesh pointed to each of the tunnels in turn that led from the chamber. Axel's eyes darted from one to the other, finally settled on the widest. 'That one.' He looked around at each of the group. 'Who's coming?'

Zesh looked around too. 'It would be stupid to split up. We stick together. Here.' He sounded so sure of himself.

Axel spat at him. 'Who do you think you are? Who's going to listen to you?'

'Who's gonny listen to you?' Fiona snapped.

Axel pulled at Liam. 'C'mon!'

Zesh watched as Axel stepped towards the tunnel. Liam didn't follow him. He looked indecisive. No change there, Zesh thought with disgust. Never knowing which way to jump. Always going with who was stronger. Usually Axel. But Liam had never been in a situation like this before. None of them had.

Axel swung round. 'I said, c'mon.'

Liam stuttered. 'We should think about this, Axel.' He paused, didn't want to admit his fear. 'It's dark in there.'

More than dark, Zesh thought, black. At least here, in the main chamber, the ribbon of lights leading down the stairwell still worked.

'You've got a light on your helmet,' Axel reminded him.

'Thanks to Mr Marks,' Zesh said.

'Thanks to him we're in this situation. Thank him

116

for nothing.'

Angie jumped up then, clutched at Axel's jacket. 'Oh, Axel, don't leave. We should all stick together.'

He yanked himself away from her. 'Shut your face, fattie.'

Angie stepped back, and glanced at Zesh. Was she expecting him to say something to Axel then? But what could he say? How was he to stop him? And anyway, things would be easier if Axel wasn't here. The rest of them would listen to him.

'Go then, you seem to think you know best. Good riddance.' Zesh turned away from him.

Axel took one last look at Liam. But Liam didn't meet his gaze. Finally, Axel aimed a spit at him, and stepped into the blackness.

Fiona watched as Axel was swallowed up by the darkness, heard his footsteps echo. She felt almost relieved he was gone. He was trouble, and they had trouble enough.

'Get me out of here, God! I promise I'll stop smoking.' She looked at Zesh. 'Who do you pray to?'

He was kneeling beside Mr Marks and he looked up at her. 'I pray to God too.'

'I thought it was Allah you prayed to.'

'Allah is God,' Zesh said, remembering now that it had been a long time since he had prayed to him.

'Well, I'm not taking any chances. I'm praying to both of them.' She closed her eyes. 'God, Allah, please get us out of here.'

She felt Angie touch her hand. 'Maybe we should all kneel in prayer?'

Why did she always have to talk so much rubbish? Fiona pulled her hand away. 'What do you think this is? One of them revival meetings?' She was shouting, her voice echoing through the chamber.

Liam looked around as if he was following the path of her voice. 'Maybe Axel will find a way out. He's got a great sense of direction,' he said, 'and then come back and get us.'

'If Axel finds a way out, he'll leave. Nelson Mandela he ain't.' Fiona looked at Liam as if she was seeing him for the first time. Was he really so stupid? Axel looked after Axel. Always had and always would.

'It was just that Mr Marks told us that some of these tunnels lead to a sea cave on the coast. There's got to be a way out.'

'And some of them don't,' Zesh reminded him, coldly.

'And we're not experts. It would be just our luck to pick the wrong tunnel,' Fiona said. Liam looked towards the tunnel that Axel had gone through. 'Follow him if you want,' she dared him. 'But I know I'm staying here.'

Angie moved beside her, almost defiantly. 'Yes, me and Fiona are staying here with Zesh.'

Fiona turned on Angie, taking her so much by surprise her eyes flashed. 'Look, Angie hen. I'm staying here because I want to stay – and not because Zesh, or anybody else suggested it. Right! I don't ever do anything to please other people. Right!'

Angie didn't say anything. It was Zesh who answered her. 'You can say that again.'

CHAPTER 14

Axel had never known anything could be so black. It was like being surrounded by night. He fumbled for the switch on his helmet and a beam of light illuminated the tunnel. Somehow, that was even worse than the total blackness. What horrors lurked on the edges of that light, just out of his vision? Creeping alongside the walls of the tunnel, ready to spring out at any moment. He stood still, listening. He could hear Fiona shouting – he couldn't make out what. He just wished that she would keep on shouting. So he would know that they were nearby.

He let out a yell as something scuttled across his foot. Had he kicked a loose stone? Was it a mouse? A rat? A giant rat? He swung round, sure that at any moment he would see eyes, bright and red and evil, watching him.

Or ... could it be the Worm? He took a step back,

imagining it sliding closer to him. Did worms have eyes? This Worm could have anything. No one had seen it. His imagination could turn it into anything. It could be dressed in a frilly frock. He tried to laugh at the picture that conjured up. Trying to stop himself being so afraid.

Shut up! He yelled it silently to himself. It was only a story. A legend, it wasn't true. And why should he be so afraid anyway? He'd been thumped by a succession of his mother's boyfriends and he'd never let any of them see he was afraid. He'd been locked up in the dark so many times and he'd refused to cry. He wouldn't be afraid now.

But before, he'd always been locked up in a room, in a house, with traffic noises outside, and people passing his windows. Here there was nothing.

Blackness.

Something scuttling into the shadows.

An ancient legend.

He heard a voice again. Were they calling him? He wouldn't go back if they were. No, not with Zesh bossing everyone about. He swivelled his light around.

There was nothing in this tunnel. It led nowhere, except into tiny, inaccessible, coffin-like spaces. And a memory of another tiny space he had once been confined in, a memory he had kept in some deep dark place, scratched in his subconscious, trying to get out.

And Axel began to sweat.

Mr Marks was opening his eyes, blinking, trying to focus. His gaze settled on Zesh.

'Mr Marks? Are you OK? What are we going to do? We're trapped down here.'

Mr Marks tried to sit up, but every movement seemed like agony. He turned his head to look up at the entrance. Even the top of the stairway was covered in boulders. The railing twisted and broken. He turned back to Zesh, swallowed and looked as if even thinking of the words to say was too much effort for him. 'You have to move into one of the other caves. Away from here. Dangerous. Help me.'

He was trying to stand up, but he let out a yell of agony as his foot bent over. Fiona ran to him. 'Where do we go, sir?'

'Into another cave. Wait,' he murmured.

Fiona almost cried out with relief. They were going to be OK. Mr Marks knew what to do. 'Hope I'm back in time for *The Simpsons*, sir,' she joked.

'Wait for what, sir? Help?' Angie asked.

Mr Marks was too weak even to answer. He only nodded, and Zesh could feel him struggling for every breath. Zesh knew that feeling.

'You don't think we should start heading for the sea, sir?' he asked.

He took too long to answer. Zesh could almost see his brain trying to figure out a way to tell them. The sea was too far. Miles and miles and miles of twisting tunnels and caves.

'Stay here,' the teacher said, and his voice was almost a whisper. 'They will find us.'

At that moment Axel burst out of the tunnel. His face was pale. 'That tunnel doesn't lead anywhere.' He said it as if he'd been asked.

Mr Marks was angry when he saw him. 'What did I tell you? Stay together – always stay together.'

'I'm not sitting about doing nothing. I'm getting out of here.'

Angie jumped towards him. 'Axel, Mr Marks says if we just wait here, they'll know how to find us.'

The idea of staying put didn't appeal to Axel. Mr Marks drew in a long breath. 'Down here, you're a team. Please remember that.'

His face was covered in sweat, cold, icy sweat. His

eyes began to roll back in his head. He was losing consciousness again. Zesh shook him. 'Mr Marks!'

Angie screamed. 'He's dead this time. I know it.'

'What is it with you, Angie. You keep wanting him to be dead!'

Zesh noticed the tremor in Fiona's voice. She was almost crying.

'He's blacked out, that's all,' Zesh said softly.

Fiona broke the long silence. 'Well, at least we know somebody'll come for us … sometime.'

Liam was quick to agree. 'Yeah, we stay here and wait, eh Axel?'

Axel didn't want to stay, didn't want Zesh to have been right. He turned his back on them all.

'Maybe we should have something to eat while we're waiting.' Angie looked around hopefully.

Axel suddenly roared with laughter. It was funny the way the sound carried through these caves, bouncing and rebounding and seeming to come back to them like a ghostly echo. 'Ha! Even here all the fattie can think about is food.'

'Shut up you!' Fiona yelled and her voice echoed too. They all stopped for a moment to listen.

'Angie's right,' Zesh said. 'We should eat something.

But not much. Maybe one sandwich, and some water. We don't know how long it'll take them to get here.'

'I'll eat how much I want,' Axel said, refusing to take orders.

Fiona refused to take orders too, but she handled it differently. 'Actually, I was just about to suggest that myself. One sandwich. Right?'

They ate quietly. Axel and Liam sat far from the rest of them, and for all his shouting, Axel did only eat one sandwich, Zesh noted.

Angie sat beside Mr Marks, wiping his face, and wetting his lips with some of her water. She's thoughtful, Zesh thought, and she hadn't panicked half as much as he expected. She looked up, caught him watching her, and she blushed.

Oh no, please don't let her think I fancy her. He looked away quickly, straight into the amused eyes of Fiona.

She grinned. He knew exactly what she was thinking. All she said was, 'Wish I had a fag.'

Zesh was just about to give her another lecture on smoking when suddenly, there was that eerie silence again. He got to his feet. Looked up at the roof. Did the stones seem looser now? Were they beginning to move again? He felt dizzy looking up, but when he looked at the rest of them they had followed his eyes and were gazing up too.

'It's moving again,' Liam said, taking a step back.

It was. Little bits of debris tumbled down, followed by a few small stones.

Then nothing, except that silence.

'Somebody help me with Mr Marks,' Zesh said. Only Fiona and Angie stepped forward. 'Let's get out of here,' he said.

Axel stood as if he was hypnotised. 'Thought you said moving on was a bad idea. Thought you were always right.'

For a moment Zesh ignored him. He was too busy trying to pull, haul, lift the dead weight of the teacher, struggling to move him into one of the tunnels. 'I was right then,' he muttered angrily,' 'and I'm right now too. We can't stay here.'

Already the rumble was beginning, a distant rumble, like thunder many miles away. But it wasn't thunder, it was an avalanche of rock hanging over them, ready to break free any second now.

'Run for it!' Zesh ordered them.

But before they could move, the lights went out.

CHAPTER 15

Angie's scream pierced Liam's eardrums. At least it sounded like Angie. He couldn't see anything. Total darkness. He wanted to scream himself. Only one beam of light ribboned the cave, like a searchlight in an air raid. Axel's. The light on his helmet reflecting his panic as it swung around them all.

Zesh's face, his eyes wide, shouting, 'Get out of here!'

Fiona, her teeth chattering.

Angie, who couldn't stop screaming.

'Shut it! Shut it!' Axel was yelling at her, but his voice was almost a scream too.

Suddenly the beam flashed on Liam, so bright he covered his eyes. 'Put your light on!' Axel shouted.

Liam fumbled for the switch while Axel's light swung up to the roof. The rocks above them were straining. 'I'm out of here!'

Zesh shouted at him, 'Help us with Mr Marks!'

Axel swore at him. 'Leave him!'

Even in that panicked moment, his words stunned them all. Angie stopped screaming.

'We're not leaving him.' It was Fiona who came forward. Her face, caught in Liam's light, was as pale as a ghost. 'Help us !' she said.

Liam ran to her automatically, hardly thinking. Expecting any second for a thunder of rock to come down on them.

'Which tunnel?' Axel shouted, but Liam felt he was talking to himself, not asking. His light flashing from one tunnel to another.

'That one,' Zesh said, and he pointed to one that sloped down. 'Mr Marks said, we go down to get to the sea.'

They half dragged, half carried the teacher. Axel unhitched the iron chain that barred their way to the tunnel and stood at the entrance. He made no move to help them. But he didn't want to go on by himself. Was that why he waited? Bet it was, Liam thought. Not such a hard man now, eh Axel?

The teacher was moaning now, trying even through his unconsciousness to help them. Groaning in agony with every move.

Angie was gasping with fear, but she was helping too.

'Come on. Quick!' Liam saw in the gleam of his lamp Axel's frightened eyes looking up. Liam followed his gaze and his beam too swung up to the roof.

At that same second, like a dam bursting, the rocks exploded. The noise was like another explosion. Angie screamed again. This time so did Fiona.

They lifted the teacher. Where did they get the strength? Fear gave them the strength, Liam was thinking. Was he thinking at all? All he knew was that he didn't want to die.

Zesh threw himself deep into the tunnel, hauling the teacher with him. Liam rolled in and fell against Fiona. She dragged a hysterical Angie behind her. The rocks rained down. It was as if the cave outside had come alive.

'It's never going to stop!' Angie screamed the words out, clamping her hands over her ears.

She was right. It was never going to stop.

Axel was jumping about like a wild man. 'It's all his fault! He should never have taken us here!'

Zesh was quiet, as if he couldn't believe this was all really happening.

As suddenly as it had started, it stopped. The last rocks hurtled on to the chamber floor, debris crashed and trickled, and then all was quiet. Liam waited for a moment, then he shone his light back into the chamber. But there was no chamber now. There was no path leading to the entrance. This fall had blocked everything. There was no chance of anyone breaking their way into them from there. They would need more than dynamite now.

'We really are trapped,' Liam said to Zesh.

Zesh didn't say anything for a while, a long while. No one did. Not even Axel. He was slumped in a corner, his head in his hands. Zesh's voice was quiet when he did speak. 'There is a way out. Mr Marks told us.' He looked at Liam. His face was ghostly in the glow of his lamp. Blackness all around him. This is like a horror film, Liam was thinking, and now we're all going to be picked off one by one.

'These tunnels lead to the sea.'

Axel jumped to his feet. 'And do you know which one leads to the sea?' He waved his hands around at the tunnels, one, two, three, four, that led from this one. 'We'll get lost.'

Zesh shrugged that off. 'We don't have any choice now. We have to move on. We'll follow the most used path. Right?'

'We should leave markers in case we have to find our way back.' This was Fiona. 'Mr Marks told us we should do that. And I saw it in a film once on telly. Never thought I'd have to actually do it myself.' She giggled. She actually giggled. 'And they say television's bad for you.'

Axel stood above the teacher. 'We're not taking him.'

Zesh was shaking his head. 'We can't just leave him here.'

Fiona stood and faced Axel defiantly. 'Look, I know it's everybody's dream, to get their own back on a teacher, but talk sense. He would die.'

Axel lifted his shoulders in a shrug. 'So?'

'We're taking him,' Zesh said.

'Well he's no' holding me back. It's his fault we're here.'

'Shut up, Axel,' Fiona said. She threw herself on the ground. She looked just about ready to cry. Her lip quivered, but she held it in. Angie was crying softly, clutching Mr Marks's hand. Zesh just looked sick.

I've never seen any of them like this, Liam thought, ready to scream. We're in terrible trouble. How are we going to get out of here?

Fiona didn't know for how long they were sitting there. Too long. She was shaking inside, scared of the dark, of the dark corners. Scared of what might happen. Refused to think that far ahead.

She could hear Zesh drawing in long breaths, Angie sobbing softly. She fumbled for the switch on her lamp. Its beam flashed on Liam, standing at the far side of the tunnel, hugging himself. He was useless, she thought. He could do nothing, always waiting around for someone to tell him what to do. Axel was looking for an easy escape. She hated to admit it, but she could only rely on Zesh. Zesh! Arrogant zonking Zesh. But arrogant or not, he was at least trustworthy, which was more than she could say for Liam or Axel. Sir zonking Lancelot. She tried to think where they could go. Down. Mr Marks's words echoed in her brain. Down to the sea. The sea cave. They had to find it. Had to!

They were all so quiet, all thinking their own thoughts.

Move. Fiona realised she was breathing as hard as Zesh. She wanted to ask him what to do, but she'd never ask anyone that. She knew as much as he did. She would ask no one.

'We can't stay here,' she heard herself say. 'We have to find this sea cave.'

Axel spat out the words. 'Right, then, lead on MacDuff.'

'If we come up against a wall, we come back, go down the next tunnel. That's why we leave the markers. Isn't it, Zesh?' Angie looked at Zesh, appealing.

But Angie had figured all that out by herself. Fiona watched her. She looked like a bloated frightened fish with tears streaming down her cheeks.

'I say we dump the teacher!' Axel snarled.

Fiona sighed. Why did he always have to act like a punk. Even now.

'I'm no' carrying him.' She noticed that his hands were balled tightly into fists. Axel was afraid, she thought. But then, weren't they all?

'I wonder if we could make some kind of stretcher out of the frame of his rucksack?' Zesh began taking it off the teacher. 'We might be able to carry him better.'

Fiona watched him as he took the frame apart and worked at it. When it was finished, it wasn't much of a stretcher, more like a pull-along sled, but it did make lifting him easier for them.

Fiona wondered why Zesh was so quiet. Was he scared? He'd never admit to that, but he had every right to be. They all had. Liam stood beside Axel. What a wimp! Even here, in this place, he was still afraid to go against him.

She turned to Angie and spoke to her sharply. She couldn't help herself. The fat girl was stupid and annoying. Why did she have to keep on sobbing? That wasn't helping anybody.

'Here, give us a hand. If we've got to pull him, we will.'

Zesh looked around the tunnels, trying to decide which one to choose. It was Axel who spoke. 'That one,' he said. He pointed. 'The sea's in that direction.'

'How do you know that?' Zesh asked him.

Axel shrugged. He pointed above. 'When we came in the entrance, the Doon was away ahead, and to the left of us.' Then he said again with assurance, 'The sea's in that direction.' He stepped inside the tunnel first. 'Right, come on then.' His voice was shaking. Behind the bold words and the anger, he was scared.

They were all scared, Fiona thought. Will we ever get out of here? And inside, she began to shake.

CHAPTER 16

Here he was, trailing behind Axel again. Nothing ever changed, did it? Even down here, trapped and scared, Liam was doing what everyone expected. Following. He was mad at himself, but too afraid to do anything to change things.

Axel had refused to help with Mr Marks, making it a real struggle for them to half drag, half carry his limp body in the makeshift stretcher through the caves. Instead, he was striding ahead, his beam of light forging a path for them through the darkness. It might have looked as if he was the leader, but deep down he knew, perhaps they all knew, that Zesh was in charge.

Were they going the right way? Liam didn't even want to think about that. Because the wrong way might lead them to …!

'Hey, how about a song!' he shouted. His voice sounded shaky and frightened. But anything was better than thinking. He had a feeling they all felt the same, for they immediately agreed.

'Good idea, Liam.' He might have known fat Angie would sound enthusiastic. If she mentioned once more she was a Girl Guide, he would scream.

'What'll we sing?' Zesh asked. His voice sounded breathless, and again Liam remembered the inhaler.

'Away and zonk yourself. I'm not singing camp fire songs.'

'You canny sing anyway.' Axel turned and burst into the conversation. 'I've heard you. Remember, Fiona? Karaoke at the school disco?'

Liam suddenly laughed. So did Zesh. They all remembered now. Fiona giving her all at the microphone, belting out a Spice Girls' song, then being pelted with sandwiches and cakes when she finished.

She remembered too. 'That wasn't my fault. The equipment was out of tune.'

That sent them all off laughing again. All except Angie. She wouldn't remember. She'd only come to the school recently. She was a bit of a mystery, was Angie. She hadn't made any friends – unless she genuinely

136

believed Fiona was her friend. No one really knew anything about her. Liam swung his light on her face, and she blinked and held her hand in front of the light

'You want me to start?' she said, and before anyone could stop her she began to sing.

They had been treated, or tortured, depending on your thinking, by Angie's singing once before. On that hill walk just a few days ago. Just a few days ago? It seemed a lifetime away now. But when she began to sing Liam still couldn't believe it. Angie sang like an opera singer. In a high soprano voice. Very posh. She belted out, 'When you walk through a storm …'

Liam caught Fiona in his light. Her mouth was wide open. She stuck out her tongue and pretended to cut her throat.

Axel screeched out. 'Is that supposed to cheer us up! That's awful. Who do you think you are, Pavarotti? Just because you're built like him.'

That suddenly sent them all into fits of laughter.

Angie was cut off just as she was urging them not to be afraid of the dark. Liam was amazed, not so much by Angie's singing, as by the fact that Axel actually knew who Pavarotti was.

'What are you all laughing at?' Angie asked innocently.

Zesh laid down Mr Marks. He was laughing so much, not just at Axel's joke but at Angie's singing, and it was making him even more breathless. He was covering up his weakness with that laughter. Didn't want anybody to know. Especially didn't want Axel to know.

'You're priceless, Angie,' Zesh said. And Angie beamed with pleasure, almost lighting up the dark cave with her bright face. It's really hard to insult her, Liam thought. She forgets insults so easily. Not like him. Liam never forgot.

Angie flopped down beside Zesh, still beaming. 'Are we going to rest now, Zesh?'

Fiona yelled across to her, 'What are you asking him for?' But she sat down too. 'If I want to rest, I rest. I don't ask anybody.'

'I think we need a leader. And Zesh is naturally the leader.' Angie had decided. Zesh could tell by her tone.

Zesh didn't say anything to that. Couldn't. He was trying too hard to get his breath back. Anyway, he knew someone who would have something to say. Axel. He came towards them. 'What makes him so special? How am I not the leader?'

Fiona guffawed. 'Oh aye, Axel. You. The boy who's

in training to be a serial killer. Oh yes, everybody'll follow you.'

Zesh took a long breath. 'I'll tell you what, Axel. It's a democracy. We'll take a vote on it … and then I'll decide, OK?'

He had meant it to be funny, but he could see that Axel didn't see the joke. He was nodding. 'As long as we get a vote,' he said.

They ate another sandwich, rationing them out, not knowing how long they could be trapped down here. Zesh longed to have the nerve to pull out his inhaler and use it. It shouldn't matter now that anyone knew. Yet here, in this dire situation, he felt it was more important than ever to keep his secret. Leaders should never show their weakness, his father had told him. And it seemed to Zesh that leadership had been thrust upon him.

Fiona spat something on to the ground. 'What's in these sandwiches? They're zonking awful.'

'I think it's the pesto sauce,' Angie's voice came from the shadows.

Fiona shone her light on her open sandwich. 'It's green,' she said in disgust.

'Mmm, lovely, isn't it?' Angie munched as if she had

never tasted anything better.

'Who made them?' But Fiona already knew the answer to that.

'Mrs Soames,' Liam said. 'She probably put poison in them after what –' he almost said, 'I', 'after what somebody did to her.'

And there in the dark, Zesh remembered the legend she had told them. He remembered the Worm. He knew from the silence that fell around him that they were all remembering the Worm. And the cook's ominous words. 'When you're deep down in those dark caves, you'll remember about the Legend of the Great Worm, and you'll be afraid then all right.' Almost as if she was prophesying that this would happen.

'It's just a stupid story,' Liam said, as if they had all been talking about it. 'It's rubbish.'

'Course it is,' Fiona agreed.

'There's more natural things to be frightened of down here. Like caves collapsing, and shafts filling with water, and rats.'

'Thanks for those cheery words, Zesh,' Fiona snapped at him.

He *had* meant it to cheer them up. Surely they were less terrifying than what they had been thinking.

'I read a book once –' Axel began, taking them all by surprise.

Fiona interrupted. 'You? A book? One of those papery things with words written on it? I am gobsmacked!'

Zesh was surprised too.

Axel glared at her, but he went on. 'It was about miners that had been trapped down a mine. They never found their way out. They became like animals, like cavemen.'

'So, how did they survive? There's nothing to eat down here. Did they bring sandwiches as well?' Fiona laughed again.

'They began to eat each other,' Axel said flatly.

Angie began to gag. 'I could never do that.'

Axel laughed now. 'We could survive on you alone, Angie, for years.'

Fiona jumped to her defence. 'We're not going to start eating Angie and that's final!' She went to her and sat beside her. 'Don't worry, Angie, I won't let anybody eat you.'

Zesh almost laughed too. It was Fiona's fault, she was so funny at times.

'What time is it, anyway?' Fiona trained her light on

her watch. 'This thing's broke.'

Zesh looked at his watch. The face was cracked and the hands still. Broken during one of the landslides, he supposed. Angie didn't have one on, and he was sure Axel still couldn't tell the time.

'Mine too,' Liam said.

And that chilled Zesh more than anything else. More than being trapped down here. More than the dark, more perhaps, than the legend of the Worm.

None of their watches was working.

* * *

'I attended school on this island. In a private school for the very elite, before the war.' The Captain offers me this information before I have asked for it.

We have stopped to rest and have water, water which runs down the rock, caught in our cupped hands.

'You have friends here, sir?'

Stupid question, for who would be friends with a man of such cruelty? Once I saw him throw a dog over the side of the ship and watch it drown, taking bets on how long it would last in the sea. Why did I not have the courage to jump in and save the poor struggling animal? But I didn't. And neither did anyone else.

This man does not make friends.

142

'Stupid people!' is all he says. 'I will now tell you a secret, Lothar. Our mission in coming here was to discover what is in these caves. The Reich believes that this is a top secret location, and here they are building a new kind of weapon. Our mission was to destroy these caves.'

'Here? But surely, sir, a top secret location for weapons would have soldiers guarding it. Here, there is nothing.'

Stupid people maybe, but surely not that stupid.

'They are a gullible people. They protect it with stories, legends to keep people from the caves.'

I began to shiver. Is it cold, or fear? 'What legend, sir?'

And then he tells me the Legend of the Great Worm which had its lair in these caves. An enormous creature, with ravenous jaws that swallowed up anyone who intruded into its underground world.

'Do not look so afraid, boy. It's a story, a made-up story. Do you want your Führer to be ashamed of you?'

I do not care if he is ashamed of me or not. He is not the one deep in this dark cave, with an ancient legend cloaked around his shoulders.

The Captain stands up. 'We move on. We may find something interesting in here.'

I am afraid now we may find something terrifying.

*   *   *

They all slept. Axel by the mouth of the cave, Liam close beside him. Angie close beside Zesh, and too close for his liking. As soon as she was sleeping he moved away from her.

Fiona was sure she would never sleep. Not here, with dangers lying in every dark corner. But she did. She closed her eyes and in just a few minutes she was snoring. As if she was sleeping comfortably in her own bed. But her dreams were dark. She was running through a ghost train at the fair, trying to find the way out, and behind her, close behind her, she could hear the slithering and the squishing of the Great Worm. But when she did dare to glance back, the face of the Worm was Angie's, bright and smiling, and just as scary. The Worm was calling her. 'Fiona. Fiona.'

Her eyes snapped open and she almost screamed. The great, fat face of Angie zoomed close to her. Too close.

'Fiona ...' she whispered.

Fiona shrank back. 'What is it?' Still a little caught up in her dream.

Angie leaned closer. Her voice became even softer. 'I'm dying for the toilet, Fiona.'

Suddenly, Fiona realised that she hadn't been to the

toilet for ... how long? Too long.

'What are we're going to do?' Angie asked her.

Fiona was thinking. 'In there can be the boys' toilet, and that one the girls' toilet.' She pointed out two tunnels leading from the cave.

'I can't go in there on my own.'

'What? Do you think the boys should come with us?'

Angie clutched at her arm. 'I'd die if they knew I needed the toilet.'

No wonder Angie drove her bonkers. 'Everybody's got to do the toilet, Angie. It's a well-known fact.'

However, even she had to admit that she wouldn't want Axel playing any of his cruel practical jokes on them in the dark of a cave. 'We won't wake them up,' she said, and she got to her feet quietly. Angie clutched on to her tightly.

Fiona shone her light into the tunnel, and they stepped gingerly inside. Did it lead anywhere? It didn't seem to. It curved around and then opened up into another cave.

'This'll do,' Angie said. Fiona hoped it would. It gave her a creepy feeling.

She'd never done the toilet so fast in her life. Her imagination was going haywire, spiders crawling the floor, armies of insects, rats ... or ... even worse. She talked all the time to keep her mind off it. 'So where did you originally come from, Angie?'

Angie was breathing hard. Fiona couldn't see her in the dark, but she knew she was close beside her. All she could see was her beam moving rapidly all round the tunnel in a panic, from the roof to the floor and back to the roof again. 'I moved here with my parents. We move all the time.'

'And why is that? You on one of these witness protection programmes? I saw that on a soap once.'

Angie giggled nervously. 'No, of course not. We never settle in one place for long. And everywhere I go, things seem to happen. Maybe I'm a jinx.'

And Fiona remembered her story about her last trip, wanted to ask her more, but not here in this dark place.

'So why do you keep moving?' Hey, you've not been expelled from everywhere else? Is that it? Known troublemaker, bully?'

That made Angie giggle. If Fiona had been prone to giggle, she might have joined in, because the thought of beaming, enthusiastic Angie ever getting into trouble was ludicrous.

'Actually, it's really bad luck that we always have to

move,' Angie said.

Bad luck and Angie? Yes, that sounds right. 'I can't wait to hear this story.' Fiona was beginning to think story-telling was something Angie had a knack for. She always had one to tell. Whether they were true or not was another matter.

Angie missed the sarcasm in Fiona's voice. She was ready to tell all.

She didn't get a chance.

'Fiona … what's that up there?'

Fiona followed Angie's beam to the roof of the tunnel. The light flickered across it. She held her breath. She felt Angie step close beside her.

The roof was moving.

CHAPTER 17

'What is it?' Angie's words came out in whispered gasps. Her eyes never left the roof.

'I don't know, and I'm not staying to find out.' Fiona began edging her way out, pulling Angie with her.

'IN CASE OF EMERGENCY MAKE YOUR WAY CALMLY TO THE NEAREST EXIT.' Isn't that what notices always said? In planes, in trains, everywhere. They hadn't reckoned on this kind of emergency.

The roof moved again. Something fluttered up there. In that same instant Fiona and Angie realised exactly what was 'up there', and Fiona forgot about remaining calm.

'BATS!'

Their screams echoed high, and the roof came alive.

They screamed as they ran, back into the cave where the boys were. The girls' screams brought them abruptly awake. Their screams, and the flapping sound of a thousand wings.

'BATS!' Fiona yelled at them. Axel rolled into the next cave. Liam, with only a second's glance at the bats, followed him.

Zesh jumped to his feet. The bats were all around him. The cave was alive with them. 'Mr Marks.' He shot to the ground beside the teacher, tried to shake him back to consciousness.

'Leave him!' Fiona shouted, running after Axel.

But Zesh couldn't. She could see that in his face. Even panic-stricken, he still wanted to be Sir Lancelot.

'Cover him with something.' Angie threw a jacket over his face. 'We have to get out of here!'

The bats were flying everywhere. Fiona threw her arms about wildly as she ran. She tripped over a rock, fell headlong forwards, covered her head with her hands, sure at any moment the bats would smother her, suck her dry.

Feet ran past her. Angie's darting light steps. Light as a feather. Funny, especially with her being so fat. Even in her terror, Fiona could think that.

Someone was screaming. Fiona realised it was herself. She couldn't stop. She would never stop. They'd never get out of here, and what other horrors would they have to face? No wonder she kept screaming.

After an age, the flapping of the wings moved into a distant cave, although the echoes remained for a long time.

'They're gone,' Zesh said, his voice shaking.

Fiona risked a look. Zesh was lying by the teacher. She tried to sit up, but she was shaking so much she could only drag herself to a wall, lean against it.

'You OK?' she asked Zesh. He nodded. 'What about him?' She meant Mr Marks, but she couldn't bring herself to say his name. This *was* his fault. He always said he would get his own back on them – but she didn't think he would be rotten enough to die on them just to get his revenge.

'He's cold, but he's sweating buckets,' Zesh said.

Axel and Liam stepped warily back into the cave.

'Thanks so much for staying here and protecting us, Axel. As usual, look after number one.' Fiona glanced at Liam as if he was dirt. 'Didn't expect anything else from you either.'

'Good job we did go in there.' Liam pointed back at the cave. 'Axel's found the way out.'

Zesh got to his feet. 'Did you? The way out?'

'It's a path, well used, leads down into a bigger cave.'

They all breathed easier. 'The way out!' Fiona jumped up. 'I wish I had a fag to celebrate.'

'Where did you go earlier?' Axel asked Fiona.

Angie answered quickly. 'Me and Fiona were looking for another way out too.' She said it quickly. 'That's what we were doing in that tunnel. Isn't that right, Fiona?'

'Were we zonks!' What was wrong with that Angie! Everybody had to do the toilet. It was perfectly natural. 'We needed the lavvy.' She said it as coarsely as she could, just to embarrass her.

'Fiona!' Angie's voice was full of disappointment in her.

'We went there for some privacy … and a thousand pairs of eyes were clocking us!'

'No wonder you frightened the bats. Seeing you two doing the toilet would scare anybody.' Axel laughed.

'They were probably more frightened of us than we were of them,' Angie said.

Fiona burst out laughing. 'You didn't think that when you and me were in there with our knickers at our ankles.'

'Oh Fiona!' There was even a blush in the way Angie said it.

Axel joined in. 'Is it a bird. Is it a plane! Come on, boys, let's get out of here! It's Angie and Fiona peeing.'

And they were all laughing. Axel and Liam and Zesh and Fiona. Even Angie. Laughing almost hysterically. Their laughter winding its way deep into the caves.

'What was that?' Liam said, his laughter stopping abruptly.

They all stopped and listened.

'An echo,' Zesh said, as if he knew.

But none of them laughed after that.

Because to them all it had sounded like something stirring, deep in the underworld.

* * *

What is that sound?

Whoosh! Something far away, a slither, a slide, coming closer.

We both stop, listening in the darkness.

The Captain dismisses the sound. 'There are always sounds in caves – echoes from the sea.'

'I am so cold, sir,' I tell him.

He looks angry. His eyes are blue and icy. 'Then be cold. We will find out where these secret weapons are, and we shall destroy them. That is our mission.'

He talks about our 'mission' as if we had been sent by God.
'We will blow this whole island to Hell. And we will die
for the Führer.'

* * *

They had been walking for hours, Axel was sure of it. How long had they been trapped down here? Hours, days? He'd lost track of any kind of time. His legs ached and his temper was growing frayed. He kept glancing behind him. Dragging that stupid teacher was holding them back. They could have been out of here an age ago if it hadn't been for him.

This had to be the way out, he was thinking. This path was worn. Many feet had passed here before them. It didn't even seem so dark here. Had his eyes got used to the blackness? Or was there some kind of artificial light in here? Water trickled down the rock walls. It was as if the water had been tinted. He tried to remember what Marks had said, something about mineral deposits colouring the water. Maybe that was what was giving off the little light they seemed to have.

I bet Zesh would know, he thought. Or pretend he does. Him and all his rules. Insisting they mark their path, making them use their whistles regularly in case someone was already in the caves searching for them, rationing their food and their use of the lamps, in case the batteries wore out. Axel wouldn't ask him anything. He hated Zesh more now than he ever had. When they got out of here, he was going to punch his lights out.

Zesh called out then, 'I think we should rest soon. Keep our strength up.'

Axel turned on him. 'We'd be out of here by now if you weren't carrying him.' He spat in the direction of the teacher, missing him by inches. 'Leave him, I say. We can send somebody back for him.'

Angie stepped forward. 'But what if the bats come back, Axel?'

'He's not got any blood for them to suck.' He sniggered at his own joke.

Liam edged closer to Axel. 'Couldn't one of us stay with him?' He looked at Zesh.

Axel liked that idea. 'Good thinking, Liam. That gets rid of two birds with one idea. You stay with him, Zesh. We'll send somebody back … eventually.'

'We are not separating. We're all staying together.'

Fiona leaped into the conversation. 'Hey, wait a minute. Just stop deciding what I'm gonny do. I'll decide for myself.'

'Who cares?' Axel said. 'Come on, Liam. You and

me, we'll just go on ourselves. Forget about them.'

He watched Liam think about it. Think too long.

It was Zesh who broke the silence. 'For once in your life, Liam, make a decision. Your backside must be sore from sitting on the fence.' He looked breathlessly angry. 'Axel won't go on his own. He's too scared.'

'I am not!' Axel yelled.

'Yes you are. Or else you would never have waited for the rest of us.'

'I'm gonny make you sorry you said that.'

Zesh ignored that. 'You are so stupid, Liam. You can't even see that he needs you more than you need him. He treats you like an idiot, and you let him. You make me sick. You've always made me sick. I can't stand people like you.'

It was turning into a tirade against Liam. It even shut Axel up.

'What have I ever done to you?' Liam asked him, taken aback.

But Zesh had started now and wouldn't stop. 'Do you know what people think about you at school? Nothing. They don't even remember you. "Liam who?" they'll say. You are a nothing. A nonentity! Because you just follow on with whoever you think is the boss. Taking orders, doing what you're told. Do you never get sick of yourself?'

Axel could see Liam's eyes flash. Was that anger, or embarrassment? Then, Liam laughed. 'You know, sometimes when you sit on the fence you can see both sides of the argument.'

Zesh turned from him in disgust. 'Oh, do what Axel tells you. That's all you're good for.'

Liam was still grinning. 'What got up his nose?'

Axel looked at him in amazement. 'See, if anybody spoke to me like that, I'd go through him.'

Liam shrugged his shoulders. 'You know me, Axel. Laugh it off, that's my motto.'

Angie was bending over the teacher, holding a bottle of water to his lips. He stirred and began to cough.

That made them all alert. 'Mr Marks!' Angie leaned closer to him. His eyes fluttered open. He looked around. Angie jumped to her feet. 'He's waking up. Everything'll be fine now.'

Axel stepped towards him. Mr Marks's eyes fastened on him. But Axel knew he couldn't see him. He couldn't see anything. 'He's still unconscious,' he said. He'd seen enough people being knocked out to recognise the signs. He was right. Seconds later the teacher's eyes closed again and his head slumped.

'Maybe we shouldn't be moving him anyway,' Axel said, as if he cared.

He didn't fool Fiona. 'We've not got much choice, have we? If we kill him because we move him, we kill him. We can't leave him here.'

Zesh stood up. 'I'm going down one of the tunnels to see where it leads.' He held out his whistle. 'I'll whistle every few minutes, and you whistle back.'

'You can't go on your own, Zesh,' Angie said.

Zesh looked around them all, as if deciding who he could ask to go with him. Axel, he dismissed right away. He'd never trust him in the dark. He hardly bothered to glance at Liam. He wouldn't be able to rely on him. And Fiona? She'd probably tell him to go zonk himself, she wasn't coming anyway.

'I'll go with you, Zesh.' Angie beamed at him.

'Aye,' Fiona laughed. 'Take Angie. You'll be all right there, Zesh. She's a Girl Guide.'

He looked at Angie reluctantly. 'I suppose,' he said without enthusiasm. 'I'll be back as soon as I can.'

'Missing you already!' Fiona called, ignoring Angie's wave.

And Zesh and Angie disappeared into the black tunnel.

'I hate that guy,' Axel muttered.

Liam glanced over at Fiona. She was ignoring them both, slugging her water from her bottle, glancing around her, checking for more bats, probably.

Liam's voice was soft. 'He wouldn't be such a big man if he didn't have that inhaler.'

Axel turned on him. 'What inhaler?'

'Didn't you know he's got asthma? Keeps it well hidden of course. Can't have anybody knowing big man Zesh has got a weakness, eh? But see if he didn't have that inhaler, Axel, he'd be as useless as ...' Liam looked over at the unconscious teacher. 'He started off as the leader as well, didn't he. And look at him now.'

CHAPTER 18

Zesh could feel Angie tugging on his rucksack as he moved steadily forwards through the cold black tunnel. 'What is it, Angie?' He sounded annoyed. Couldn't help it.

'Nothing. I'm just holding on, Zesh.'

She flashed her light along the tunnel. 'Do you think this might be the way?'

It has to be, Zesh was thinking. He couldn't think straight, yet he had to. Trying to remember all that Mr Marks had told him. He took a step forwards and jumped back quickly as rubble broke loose under his feet. He looked all around, waiting for the whole tunnel to collapse.

'I don't think this is any good here,' he said.

'If you say so, Zesh.'

He would never admit it, but he was glad it was Angie who was there with him. She didn't moan or argue. She just followed quietly. And he didn't want to be alone.

'You're probably wishing you'd never come to this school.' He wanted to talk, to hear their voices in the black tunnel.

'Oh no, I love it here. Everyone's so nice.' She giggled. 'Well, maybe not everyone. But you are, and so's Fiona.'

You honestly think Fiona's nice, Angie? thought Zesh. He didn't look behind but he could imagine her face, beaming with enthusiasm.

'She's the best friend I've ever had.'

You're sad, Angie, he was thinking. If Fiona's the best friend you could ever get, you are really pathetic.

'What school did you go to before?' he asked her, realising then that he knew nothing about Angie. None of them did.

'We were abroad,' she said at once. 'My dad's got this absolutely brilliant job. He works for the government.'

Her words were cut off as Zesh grabbed at her, and tugged so hard on her arm he almost pulled her over.

'My foot's gone down a hole.' He tried to say it as calmly as he could, but he was losing his balance, and if he did, he would slip down. 'Pull, Angie. Help me.'

Angie turned her light down into a deep dark hole that had seemed at first to be just a crack in the ground. She caught her breath, gripped Zesh and hauled him back on to firm ground.

Zesh was breathing hard. 'We'll have to tell them all to be careful.'

'It's lucky for you I was here,' Angie said.

And though Zesh hated to admit it, she was right. 'Come on, we're going back.' They backed out, this time their lights scanning the floor of the tunnel for any more of these booby traps. He felt there was danger in every step. How he wished he was home.

'Do you think we'll ever get out of here?' Angie asked him.

Zesh didn't answer. In the dark he took the inhaler from his pocket and drew in a lifesaving breath.

'Was that you using your inhaler?' Angie asked.

He drew in another breath quickly, this time with shock. 'What are you talking about?'

'You do use an inhaler, don't you? It's not a secret, is it?'

Zesh waited till his breath was calm again before he answered her. 'I don't want the rest of them to know.'

Angie stepped closer. Her round face seemed to

zoom at him through the gloom. 'I would never tell on you, Zesh. Your secret's safe with me.'

Fiona heard Zesh's whistle piercing the darkness. Maybe Sir Lancelot's found the way out. She almost prayed. Axel and Liam were crouched across from her on the other side of the cave, muttering to each other. Hatching plans. Even down here, Axel was trying to act like the tough guy. It was so stupid. She wanted none of it. She wanted home. She kept looking around her. So much blackness. An eternity of blackness. Anything could be hiding in that blackness, ready to reach out, grab her, drag her back into the shadows.

Shut your face, Fiona! she told herself. She moved closer to the teacher. Though he would be of no zonking help if she was dragged off. If he would just wake up and tell them which way to go. Point a wavering finger in the right direction, then conk out again. She was so scared they were going the wrong way. That all this time they weren't heading for the sea, but going deeper into a cave with no way out.

She couldn't think about that any more. She refused to think.

'You got a fag on you, Axel?'

He snarled an answer. 'No, I have not got a fag.'

'I've got a bit of chewing gum.' Liam held it out to her.

'Chewing gum I've got,' Fiona snapped.

'You're suffering from withdrawal symptoms. That's why you're in such a bad mood,' Liam said.

Axel sniggered. 'Withdrawal symptoms nothing. She's always in a bad mood.'

'See when we get out of here, Axel, I'm going to put your time in.'

'You and what army?' Axel laughed, then he added seriously, 'You coming wi' me and Liam. 'Cause we're getting out of here. Without *him*.'

Him, was Mr Marks.

'Oh my goodness, Liam.' Fiona's voice was full of sarcasm. 'Made a decision, have you?'

'I've got my reasons,' Liam said.

Fiona thought about it. Moving faster without the teacher holding them back. Getting out. Sending help back for him. It was sensible. Yet … leaving the others alone, with bats and rats and … whatever else might be in these dark ancient caves? Could she do that?

'Oh come on, Fiona. It's not *Who Wants to Be a Millionaire?*'

'No. It's only your life,' Liam said.

They heard movements in the cave, steps coming closer, and voices. Zesh and Angie were on their way back.

Zesh was shaking his head. 'Not that way, anyway. It leads nowhere.'

Angie ran to Fiona. 'Zesh nearly fell down a hole. It was really scary.'

Fiona grinned sarcastically. It was all lost on Angie. 'Good thing you were there, eh? We might have lost him for ever.'

Zesh dusted himself down. 'We'll have to be careful where we're walking.' He peered towards the other tunnel. 'We'll try that way.'

Liam stood as if he was ready to say something. Axel held him back, but Zesh noticed.

'What's wrong?' Zesh asked him.

'Your arrogant attitude. That's what's wrong.' Axel's whole stance was threatening. 'Telling everybody what to do. As if you were still a prefect. Down here you're nothing. Remember that.'

Zesh held his stare. 'Even down here I've got more brains than you.'

Axel's eyes flashed. Liam stepped back, sure Axel would fly at Zesh. Even Zesh expected it and steeled himself. But Axel didn't. Instead he snarled dramatically, 'We'll see about that.'

Fiona stretched herself. 'Well, I'm not going anywhere now. I am shattered. It must be bedtime. At least here we can sleep for a while.'

Angie touched the teacher's face. 'Mr Marks is so cold.' She took her bottle, opened it and wet his lips. She was the only one who ever thought to do that, Zesh realised. She does all the right things, yet she still gets right up everybody's nose.

'We'll have to get him some medical help soon.' Angie looked up at Zesh, as if all her hopes of freedom depended on him. That annoyed him too. He was as scared as any of them. Why did they expect him to know everything?

'Do you know a way out, Angie? Is there a zonking lever in here somewhere that you press and it shoots us to safety?' Fiona sounded angry.

Angie's eyes filled up with tears.

'No. Didn't think so, Angie. So shut your gob.' Fiona flopped and turned her back on them all, pulled her knees up and wrapped her arms around them. Angie looked embarrassed. For once, she didn't know what to say.

'We all need some sleep,' Zesh said. He sat down beside Angie. 'Then we move on.' He nodded towards the other tunnel. 'That way.'

Axel and Liam said nothing. They sat at the other side of the cave, watching Zesh.

He could feel their eyes on him, even when he closed them. He snapped them open once, and sure enough they were still watching him.

He wouldn't sleep, he told himself. Couldn't. Not when they were watching him like that. He didn't trust them. They were up to something. Maybe, while he slept, they meant to slip off on their own.

That wasn't a threat, he realised. That was a dream. Axel was nothing but trouble. He'd be better gone. Zesh closed his eyes and slept.

Fiona was dreaming of more bats, their wings fluttering, their cries filling the caves. But these bats could talk. She could hear them swearing, shouting. She jumped awake. The noise still filled the caves, and in the gloom a rolling bundle moved towards her. Angie woke too, just as Fiona jumped to her feet.

'What's going on?'

It took her a moment to realise that the rolling bundle was Liam and Axel and Zesh. Liam and Axel were holding Zesh down. Zesh's face was bleeding where one of them had punched him – Axel probably. They hauled Zesh to his feet. Axel felt in Zesh's pockets, pulled something out with a triumphant yell. 'Gotya!'

He held it aloft for them all to see. Like a trophy won by a warrior. An inhaler?

Zesh struggled to try to snatch it from him, but Axel was too strong. He pushed Zesh back so hard he stumbled and fell. Axel spat at him.

'See, who's got the brains now? Eh! Tell me that! Who's got the brains now!'

CHAPTER 19

Axel got to his feet, stood over Zesh and pushed him back on to the ground with his boot. Zesh was white around the lips.

Fear. Axel recognised it. Not so bossy now, was he? He looked over at Liam. 'I think he knows who's in charge now, eh?' Liam grinned back.

Fiona ran towards them. 'What's going on here!'

Axel told her. 'I'm fed up wi' him.' He poked at Zesh with his foot again. 'Telling everybody what to do. Telling me what to do. Now I've got this.' He showed her the inhaler. 'He'll not boss anybody about again.'

She tried to snatch it from him. 'Axel, give him it back. That's rotten.'

She looked at Zesh, expecting him to do something, but Zesh was stunned. Still couldn't believe it. The fight was out of him.

'Zesh!' Fiona shouted. 'Don't let him get away with this.'

But Zesh said nothing.

Axel took the inhaler and pushed it deep inside the pocket of his jacket. He patted it. 'And that's where it's going to stay. You behave yourself, Zesh, and I might just let you have it back. But no back chat, no cheek, and it's my rules from now on.'

He said the last bit with relish. Rolling it around his tongue, taking his time to spit it out. My rules from now on.

'And we're not going to have anybody hold us back.' Axel looked down at Mr Marks. 'And that means him.'

'We can't leave him behind,' Zesh said.

'You carry him then … oh forgot, you'll not be able to breathe.' Axel moved close to his face. 'It's your choice, Zesh. You carry him if you want, but I'm not helping him and neither is he.'

Zesh looked at Liam as if he had just crawled out from under a rock. 'Come off the fence at last, have you, Liam?'

'Know what side my bread's buttered on, don't I?' Liam licked his lips nervously. 'Anyway, we're going to send somebody back for him.' He looked at Axel. 'So we will, Axel?'

Axel didn't answer him.

Angie stepped closer to Zesh. 'I'll stay with Zesh,' she said firmly.

Then, a startling thing happened. Zesh turned on Angie furiously, taking all his anger out on her. 'You! You keep well back from me. You said you wouldn't tell. But the first thing you do when you get back here is tell him, of all people. Typical fat Angie. You couldn't keep your mouth shut, could you!'

Angie almost fell back with the shock. Her hand flew to her mouth. Axel's laugh filled the whole cave.

'At last, no more Mr Nice Guy Zesh. Fat Angie, he called her!'

Angie was trying to mumble something but she couldn't get the words out. She looked at Fiona. 'Fiona, you don't think ...'

But Fiona turned her back on her too.

Axel looked at Liam and winked. Liam winked back. Good. Zesh thought it was the fat bird who had told him about the inhaler, Axel realised. Let him think that. Let them all think that. Divide and rule. Get the rest of them fighting against each other and there is only one winner. Where had he heard that? He couldn't remember. In a film, he was sure of it.

'Your choice, Zesh,' Axel said, and this time nobody said a word.

'Do you feel all right?' Fiona edged closer to Zesh. He looked miserable. She had never seen him so miserable.

He just looked at her. 'Oh, I'm brilliant. I'm an asthmatic and my worst enemy's just stolen my inhaler … oh, and I'm also trapped underground with him. Let me see … do I feel all right? What do you think!'

'Don't be so zonking cheeky!' she answered him. 'I didn't even know you had asthma, right!'

'Nobody did. Except her!' Zesh glared across at Angie, who hadn't stopped weeping since he'd turned on her. Angie was huddling close to the teacher as if he could comfort her.

'There's not a bad bone in her body,' Fiona said. 'She's just thick. She never knows when to shut her mouth.'

'Taking lessons from you, is she?'

'Hey, I'm supposed to be the comedian here. I've a good mind not to talk to you at all. I'm trying to be nice … for a change.' She hesitated. Zesh was already getting on her nerves. 'What are we going to do?'

Zesh knew what she meant. Were they going to leave the teacher here … and go on without him?

'He's right, you know,' she said. 'Axel, that is. It is stupid to carry him about with us. He's too heavy. We could be doing him more harm than good. Maybe we should just leave him.'

'Easy for you to say.' Zesh wheezed the words out painfully. He could manage without the inhaler now, but soon, he wouldn't be able to breathe without it.

'It's all in the mind,' he said suddenly, as if to himself. 'Because I've not got the inhaler, I think I need it. I don't. I'll be fine.'

He tried to take a deep breath but there was a whistle deep in his chest that gave away the pain he was already feeling.

'We could jump him,' Fiona said. Knowing they couldn't. Zesh didn't have the strength, and Axel was built like a Clydesdale horse. 'He's getting his own back on Marks, you know. Axel was scared coming here. Scared that here, Mr Marks would get him. But the tables have turned. Axel's happy now.'

Zesh wheezed, 'How could he be that bad? How could anybody?'

Fiona tutted. 'Because you *are* an arrogant zonker, Zesh.'

He glared at her. 'I need you. I really need you.'

'Don't get me wrong. Axel's a zonker as well. It's just my luck I'm trapped in hell with a bunch of zonkers.'

There was a rumbling deep below them. It made them all stop and listen. Even Angie stopped weeping and looked up.

'What was that?' Fiona's voice was a whisper.

It came again, ominous. Shuddering through the rocks.

'An earthquake?' Axel asked. 'Somewhere deep down in the earth.'

They all sat still, listening, not saying a word. Not until Angie, in a whisper, voiced all their fears.

'Maybe … it's the Worm.'

*   *   *

I do not want to die for anyone. I'm only seventeen. I want to go home. Therese is waiting for me. I dream of her. Before I left, Therese let me kiss her and she promised she would wait for me. I torture myself thinking of her forgetting me, taking up with some other boy. Though, as my mother reminds me, there are not many boys left at home.

'The postman is still single and he is looking for a wife,'

my mother jokes in her letters. 'He is only sixty-two. He would make Therese a lovely husband.'

Why am I still following this crazy man? He wants to blow up a whole island? An island filled with people he knows. Only a fanatic could do that.

So why don't I turn my back on him, and go?

Because I have been taught to obey orders, and he is still the officer.

But I am so cold, so hungry, and there are strange sounds in this cave.

CHAPTER 20

In the end, Zesh wouldn't leave the teacher behind.

'You're daft!' Axel told him. 'You'll not be able to breathe carrying him.'

But Zesh had made his decision, for now. While he could still breathe he would help carry him, and maybe by the time he couldn't, he would have his inhaler back.

Axel looked at Fiona. 'You're helping him? You hate that Marks. He was always getting at you as well.'

She didn't deny that. 'You've not got my inhaler,' she said. 'I can do what I want.'

So, they began moving ahead warily. Axel and Liam at the front, refusing to help with the teacher. Zesh and the girls behind, lifting, dragging Mr Marks on his makeshift stretcher, as best they could.

'We're probably breaking every bone in his body,' Fiona moaned.

The strain of lifting him was only making Zesh

worse. Fiona listened to his laboured breathing. 'Give him back his inhaler, Axel. This isn't doing anybody any good.'

'It's helping me,' Axel said smugly.

Angie hadn't dared speak to Zesh since he'd snapped at her. She'd been, for Angie, remarkably quiet. Now she whispered to him, 'Zesh, please don't think I told Axel about your asthma. I didn't. Honest.'

Zesh couldn't even look at her. 'Doesn't matter now. He's got it, hasn't he?'

'But I didn't tell him.'

Her whisper was more urgent now, carried through the dark to Liam. He nudged Axel, called back cheerfully, 'And if you believe that, Zesh, you'll believe anything.'

Angie gasped and fell silent again. Zesh said nothing. It was hard enough to carry the teacher. Impossible to talk as well. Especially now. Zesh was afraid. More afraid than he'd ever been. He'd had asthma attacks before. Attacks that left him clawing for breath, unable to stand up. Wishing that he could just stop breathing for a few minutes, so his lungs could rest. Knowing that breathing *is* life, and yet it was breathing that was killing him. Since his last attack he had kept it under control, promised himself he'd never be in that position again. Yet here he was, worse than he'd ever been.

'I'll be OK,' he ordered himself. He was a great believer in positive thinking. He was sure he would be fine. Breathe deeply. Don't be afraid. But his breath was catching already. His lungs were closing like the tunnels in this cave, growing smaller, tighter. NO! He would not think like this.

'Have you got a spare?' Fiona asked him.

Of course he had a spare. His mother never let him go anywhere without a spare. And where was it?

'In the drawer beside my bed at the hostel,' he said. Too many words. Too much effort.

'Not much zonking good there, is it?'

He almost smiled. She was so right. Not much zonking good there. His mother, he could see her worried face as he left, insisting he take it, telling him always to have it just in case.

But when had he ever listened to his mother?

As the caves opened below them, they found a strange new world. Here the rock had formed into fantastic shapes and patterns. Constant dripping water had caused that, Zesh remembered Mr Marks saying. In places there was rock hanging from the roof like filigree curtains. Stalactites cascading from the ceilings and forming into grottoes dramatically. It was beautiful, but Zesh couldn't appreciate its beauty for now.

Then they found themselves in another chamber, with a wall like honeycomb. Liam touched it and jumped back in disgust. The wall was slimy with age.

'What is that?' he gasped and wiped his hands frantically on his jacket. 'It's soft.' He glanced around them. 'Rock isn't supposed to be soft, is it?'

Fiona touched it too. Her face said it all. 'Whatever it is, it's spongy.' She grimaced. 'Let's get out of here.'

'Maybe it means we're near the sea. There is a lot more water here.' Liam looked around for someone to agree with him.

'Or the caves are flooding,' Zesh said, remembering the teacher's words again. How quickly caves can flood down here.

'There speaks the voice of doom,' Axel groaned. 'Don't worry, I'm getting you out of here. Me!'

Fiona pushed past him. 'I'm getting myself out of here, pal. This place is giving me the creeps.'

It seemed they all felt the same. They left that chamber almost in a panic, glad to be back in a larger cave where the air seemed clearer, the cave not so oppressive.

The chambers were larger, and walking was almost easy.

Axel came right up close to Zesh. 'Who's the one with the brains now?'

Zesh took the chance to dive at him, but he wasn't quick enough. Axel darted from his grasp with a triumphant laugh.

Suddenly Angie lunged at him too. 'I demand you give it back to him. We've got to work together to get out of here. A team, Mr Marks said.'

Axel didn't even let her finish. 'Marks doesn't have a vote now. In fact, neither do you, fattie. I'm the only one who has a vote. So sit down on your fat bum and shut up.'

Liam laughed and joined Axel. 'You've got a cheek. If it hadn't been for you Axel wouldn't even have known about the inhaler.'

She drew her breath in. 'That's not true.' She looked at Zesh. At Fiona. 'It's not true.'

Axel pushed her back. 'This never happens at Girl Guide camp, does it?'

Angie fell behind, defeated. She sat back, on her own.

Zesh didn't care any more whether she'd told them or not. He just wanted to breathe. The attack on Axel had been a bad idea. It had taken too much out of him. Must conserve my strength, he thought. He closed his eyes. I'll be OK. I'll be OK. Allah help me. I'll be OK.

Angie tugged Fiona awake. Fiona grunted in annoyance. Angie had been crying. Her eyes were red-rimmed and blotchy. 'We have to do something, Fiona, to help Zesh.'

Fiona pulled herself away roughly. 'Like what? Give him the kiss of life? You're on your own, Angie.'

'We could ask Axel together.'

'Appeal to his better nature, you mean? In case you haven't noticed, Angie hen, Axel hasn't got a better nature. You know the only thing he understands is violence. If you want something, batter somebody and take it. If you and me were to jump him, batter lumps out of him and take the inhaler off him, that he would understand. And d'ye know how, Angie? Because that's all that's ever been done to him.'

Angie was wide-eyed, listening. 'Are you trying to make me feel sorry for him?'

Fiona tutted at that. 'I don't feel sorry for him. We've all got our problems. I'm just telling you that's the way Axel is. Not everybody lives in Girl Guide land, Angie.

Look at me, my mother's a party girl. Always has been. She was always leaving me in by myself from I was a tiny wee thing. She doesn't want to get old. Still thinks she's sixteen. God knows what age she is under all that make-up she wears. I could use her as an excuse. It's all my mother's fault. What's the point? It would be lovely to have designer parents, lovely house, perfect life. But, Angie, it doesn't happen for everybody. You've just got to play the cards you're dealt with, and get on with it.'

Angie looked at her thoughtfully. 'Play the cards you're dealt with,' she repeated. 'I like the sound of that. What does it mean?'

'It means you make the best of what you've got. Stop whingeing and blaming everybody else. Get on with it, and who knows, you might win the game.'

Fiona remembered her mother telling her that one day after a teacher had lectured her on being a better mother. 'I might be useless,' she had told Fiona, 'But I'm the only one you've got. So get on with it.' Her mother might not have taught her much, but she had taught her never to feel sorry for herself. There was no sentimentality when it came to her mother. She found that was helping her a lot now.

'I think that's a wonderful philosophy, Fiona.'

Zonks, Angie did come out with some rubbish at times.

'Well, what you've said has just convinced me that I must do something to help Zesh.' Angie clutched at Fiona's arm and whispered, 'You don't believe I told Axel about Zesh's asthma?'

Fiona looked into Angie's pleading eyes. She knew deep down that Angie would never lie about such a thing. Axel must have found out some other way. But something, something wicked in her, stopped her from telling that to Angie. She was suddenly fed up with her, with her crying and her clutching, and her never-ending cheeriness.

Instead she said, 'Misfortune seems to follow you about, Angie. And you always claim it's never your fault. What about that school trip? Somebody died?' She glanced at Mr Marks. 'Zonks, Angie, if you ask me you're the Angel of Death.'

'It was a skiing accident. Nothing to do with me.' But Angie's voice wavered.

'A skiing accident? In Paris? Or was that yet another school trip from hell? I'm beginning to think you like making up stories, Angie. And now you're on this school trip, and let's face it, Angie, things couldn't be much worse, could they? But of course, that's not your fault either. It's never your fault.'

'Fiona, please, we mustn't quarrel. Not now.'

That, it seemed to Fiona, was the last straw. 'You mean, with us being best friends and everything? Angie, get it through your thick head, you are the last person I would be best friends with. You're fat and ugly and too thick to realise I cannot stand you. And when we get out of here I never want to see your fat, ugly face again!'

With every word Angie scrabbled back, away from Fiona's wrath, as if every word was a dagger stabbing into her.

'Can you get that through your zonking brain? Or do I have to draw a picture?'

With that Fiona turned her back on Angie. Maybe now, she'd get some peace.

Axel ate his chocolate and surveyed them. He liked this feeling. Power. Zesh lay against the teacher, breathing painfully. He hadn't even heard the argument between Fiona and the fat bird. That had been great. Fiona was sleeping now. Axel didn't mind Fiona. Deep down he thought of her as 'one of us'. But she needed a lesson. The fat bird was way off on her own. She wasn't sleeping. She was still crying. What a wimp. That was a smart move on Liam's part to let them all think she had been the one who'd told him about Zesh's inhaler. Now, neither Zesh nor Fiona trusted her. Divide and rule. It was working already.

He was lord of all he surveyed. What was that daft poem one of the teachers had told him about? Something about a bird. A hawk, roosting in the trees, having power over everything.

Well, that was him now.

A hawk.

CHAPTER 21

Liam could smell the sea. He was sure of it. The walls of the cave were damp. Yes, they would soon be out. The thought of not finding a way out – of staying in here for ever – he refused even to consider. Axel was wild with power and that scared him. No one would be able to control him if anyone went against him. But who would go against him now?

Certainly not Zesh. He wheezed in a corner as he dozed. His harsh breathing echoed through the dark. I should feel sorry for him, Liam told himself. But I don't. He's always been too sure of himself. And he had no right to bring me down the way he did. In front of everybody. Let him suffer just a bit longer. I mean, people don't die of asthma, do they?

Liam's eyes turned to Angie, cowering in a corner, like a beached whale, trembling from fear and hurt probably. He had heard Fiona turn on her too. About time too. Angie was a pain in the butt. No, the only one who would have the gumption to stand up to Axel would be Fiona – and she wasn't doing it. Why? Probably because she thought of Axel as her kind. He lived in her world – up there.

Up there. It was another world he was remembering. Up there on the surface.

Yet down here it was as if all the lines had been blurred, and Liam wasn't sure where Fiona stood any more.

But she'd stick with them in the end. If there was a choice to be made, Fiona would stick with Axel. She'd never choose Zesh.

Axel got to his feet. 'Right! Come on. We're moving.'

Fiona got to her feet. 'Not till you give Zesh that inhaler. Axel, listen to him. He can't breathe. You canny expect him to carry Marks like that.'

Zesh had sat up. It was too difficult for him now even to talk. His face looked pale as the light shone on him, his eyes eerie pinpoints in the gloom.

'I've got an answer to that. Leave the blinkin' teacher.' Axel lifted his shoulders. 'That's the sensible thing. That's what I've decided.'

Liam saw the sense in that too. It was impossible to take him on. Why was Zesh so insistent?

'Give him the inhaler!' Fiona took one step forward. Her face was grim. Liam wanted to see this. If Fiona lunged at Axel she'd give him a good go for his money. But she'd never win. She must know that. Axel was too powerful, built like a steamroller. And Liam wouldn't let her win. He was definitely on Axel's side now.

Axel made a stupid face at her, taunting her. 'Make me! Make me!' he chanted.

Then it happened, taking them all by surprise. It wasn't Fiona who moved. It was Angie. Out of the dark she came, lumbering, charging against Axel with a roar that sounded just like another earthquake. It took Axel so much by surprise that he didn't have time to avoid her. She pounded into him, sent him shooting backwards on to the ground. She fell on top of him, grabbed his ears and pushed his head back. No one moved. It was all happening too fast. It was like watching a movie, Liam kept thinking. This isn't real life. This isn't happening.

Axel only took a minute to pull himself together. He gripped a handful of Angie's hair. She screamed. He threw her from him and her clawing nails left a trail of blood on his face.

Axel wiped the blood with his hand. He looked at it as if he couldn't quite believe what it was. His blood. Then his malevolent eyes turned on Angie. She was stumbling to her feet.

Axel ran at her. 'I'll get you for that!' he yelled.

Fiona yelled too. 'Axel, don't!'

Angie gasped. She took a few steps back.

And suddenly, Angie was screaming. At first, Liam thought she was putting on an act, her arms flailing, and staggering as if she was having a fit. Her eyes were almost popping out of her head.

Too late he realised, all of them realised, that Angie was falling.

She reached out her hands for help. She reached out to Axel, closest to her. But no one could help. It all happened too fast, in seconds. Angie let out an ear-shattering scream of terror – and then, she was gone. Plummeting, her scream echoing, echoing, then disappearing, dying into silence.

Axel was shaking. 'I never touched her. That wasn't me!'

He looked around frantically for someone to believe him. Zesh was on all fours, crawling closer. Fiona, who had been standing like a statue, suddenly shot forwards, threw herself on the ground and began to shout through the hole.

'Angie!' She screamed it down the fissure they hadn't even seen, where rocks and debris tumbled after Angie. 'Angie!'

They all held their breath, praying for an answer.

'I warned you about holes,' Zesh said with difficulty.

'Shut up!' Axel yelled, then he flung himself down beside Fiona. 'Angie!' His voice was even louder than Fiona's. 'She's got her whistle. Shout and tell her to use her whistle.'

Fiona took her own whistle and blew it as hard as she could. But though they waited, there was no answering whistle.

'She's dead,' Liam said, hopelessly. 'She must be dead.'

Axel got to his feet. 'It wasn't my fault. She ran at me first. I never touched her.'

No one answered him. Fiona only blew her whistle again. And again.

'She can't answer you,' Liam said. 'She's dead.'

Fiona swung at him. 'Shut up about her being dead. She's not dead. Right!'

Axel tried to be funny. 'She's probably stuck somewhere. I mean she's that fat.' He didn't get another
word out. Fiona turned and slapped his face.

'That's not funny. She's maybe just unconscious.
We've got to find her.'

Axel, mad at her slap, screamed at her. 'We'll never
find her. Don't be so stupid. We've got to get out of
here.'

'I'm not going anywhere till we find her.'

'You said yourself she was a Jonah.' Axel's voice was a
yell. 'The Angel of Death, you called her. Somebody
died on the last school trip she was on.'

And they were all silent, thinking, Liam was sure of
it, the same thing. Somebody had died on this one too –
but no one had expected it would be Angie herself.

Fiona began pulling the rope from her backpack.
'I'm going down after her.'

Nothing anyone could say would stop her. Even Axel
tried. 'You'll be the one gets lost.'

Liam too. 'When we get out we'll send somebody
back for her.'

Fiona snapped at him. 'You're great for sending
people back. At this rate you'll have an army down here

looking for us.'

Zesh tried too, with hardly a breath. 'It's too danger-ous.' What he was really thinking was, it should be me going down. He was useless now.

'What if she is unconscious? And she wakes up and she's on her own, and she knows we've gone on and left her?' The thought seemed to pain Fiona. 'I'm going down and that's it. She might be on a ledge or something.'

She tied the rope around her waist and stood at the edge of the hole, shining her lamp down. Zesh wanted to ask why she was doing it. This wasn't like Fiona. This was a different Fiona. But they were all different down here, except maybe Axel.

'I'll keep whistling. You keep whistling back. That's all I'm asking.'

'You're crazy, Fiona,' Liam shouted at her.

'I'm still going.' She sounded frightened. She looked down again. Her beam only lit so far, and then it plunged into blackness.

'Nobody's coming after you if you don't come back,' Axel said angrily, his face threateningly close to hers. He's angry because she won't do what he says, Zesh thought.

Fiona pushed Axel from her. 'Nobody's asking you. Just hold on to the other end of this rope and haul me up when I give three blasts on the whistle, right.'

She looked over at Zesh and he lifted a hand to wave. He wanted to say something, to assure her he would make them wait for her, make them pull her up, but it was taking all of his strength now, just to breathe.

She took a step over the edge, looked at Axel. 'See if you don't wait for me, I'll tell your mammy, Axel … and her new boyfriend.'

Zesh wanted to laugh, but all he managed was a smile. Typical Fiona, still spouting off even at a time like this.

Her eyes found him, just for a second, and then she disappeared into the chasm.

'Angie!' Fiona yelled into the impenetrable gloom. 'Angie!' But even she could hear the hopelessness in her voice. She never would find her. As she lowered herself from one black cavern into another, she realised that Angie could have slipped through any one of them. She blew hard on her whistle and the sound screeched through the tunnels, echoed, and Fiona stopped, grabbing at ledges, searching for footholds and waited for some answer, a faint cry, an answering whistle, anything.

'Angie!' she screamed again, fighting back sobs. Thinking of her sliding down this long black tunnel, falling, perhaps lying somewhere, terrified. Was she close by, trying to call back, but, like Zesh, too weak?

Was she unconscious?

Was she …? No!

She couldn't be. Girls like Angie didn't die. No one was meant to die. It was a school trip for zonks sake. An afternoon adventure, Mr Marks had called it, going down into his beloved caves, sharing the excitement of them. Adventure? Disaster!

They were supposed to be back at the hostel now, having that disco, or was it morning already, or days later? She didn't know, couldn't tell. What had happened to time down here? That frightened her too. How long had they been down here? Were there search parties out looking for them? Was her mother worried about her? Had they contacted her in Benidorm?

And what about Angie's family? Waiting for her, not knowing that she would never be coming back. No! She would not think this way. She would come back. She had to. Because if she didn't, Fiona could never forgive herself. After all she'd said to her. She had to find her. She wasn't even afraid down here, in the dark, the way she thought she would be. She didn't think of the terrors that might lurk in these deep dark tunnels that wound their way under the island.

All she could think of was Angie.

She wasn't thinking that only Axel and Liam were up there to pull her back, and she trusted neither of them.

Or that the rope might break.

That she might be trapped down here for ever.

She wasn't even thinking of the Worm.

All she could think of was Angie.

CHAPTER 22

Fiona was shaking when she was pulled back up. Her face smudged with dirt and tears. She'd been crying, Axel thought. And she wasn't even trying to hide it. Crying for Angie? Why was she taking it so hard? Axel couldn't understand it.

'Told you you'd never find her,' was the first thing he said to her.

She snapped back at him. 'Shut up!'

She dragged herself on to the rim of the hole and untied the rope around her waist with trembling fingers. 'There's too many tunnels down there. They go everywhere. She could have slipped down any one of them.' She looked up at Axel, her voice dry with sobs. 'Where did she go?'

He pictured Angie sliding down, unstoppable, like someone on a funfair ride. Funny, if it wasn't so terrifying. He pushed the thought of it away.

'She's gone. There's nothing we can do about it. We'll move on.' He looked around at them all. At Fiona, and Liam and Zesh. 'We have to keep moving.'

Fiona didn't answer. She crawled to a far side of the chamber, curled up and began to cry again. This wasn't like Fiona. Fiona didn't do the crying thing. What was happening?

'We'll rest for a bit, then move on.' Axel wasn't asking them for an opinion. He was telling them. Liam didn't argue. He was shaking so hard Axel could almost hear his bones jangling. He was staring at the hole that had sucked Angie away from them.

'There's something in these caves, Axel. Something that's got Angie.' He turned and looked at Axel, his mouth quivering as if he was frightened to put his fear into words. 'There's something in these caves.'

*   *   *

'I am not going any further, sir.'

At last I find the courage to stand up to him. I believe he is crazy. He mutters to himself as he walks ahead of me. I believe too that he is as afraid as I am but will never admit it. He does not want to be taken prisoner, he says. A good German would rather die.

Ha! I am a good German, and I would rather live.

He turns on me. His eyes are wild with anger. 'You dare to disobey an order!'

I will not even answer that. Down here, in this strange, black underworld, I am no longer under his command. 'I am going back.'

His mouth curls into an ugly grin. 'You are lost. You will never find your way.'

But I will, though he does not know it. I have made sure I will find the way out. I turn my back on him.

His voice booms behind me. 'Take one more step and I will kill you.'

I hear the click of his gun, turn my head slowly. He stands in the shadow, I cannot see his face. All I see is the gun, pointing at me.

But he would not shoot me, surely?

For us, the war is over, for now at least. Down here there is another enemy. I am afraid to think what it is.

'I do not believe you will hurt me, sir,' I say, trying to convince him as much as myself. 'You have a son my age, you once told me. You would not shoot your own son.'

And I turn from him again.

The bullet whistles by my ear. I feel a stinging pain and throw myself on the ground. The explosion roars through the caves and I can imagine the sound going from chamber to *chamber, waking bats and rats and, maybe, somewhere deep in its lair, a Great Worm.*

I am shaking with fear as the Captain comes and stands above me, the gun still pointing at my head.

'I would not think twice about killing my son if he disobeyed an order.'

He says it and I believe him. This time, he would kill me. I am about to die.

* * *

Axel shook Fiona awake and she pulled herself free of him. 'Leave me be!' She sniffed back a tear.

'Come on, Fiona, have something to eat before we move.' He was trying to hand her a packet of crisps.

Zesh rasped to him. 'Give me the inhaler, Axel.' Every word seemed to struggle out of him.

'No way!' Axel said at once. 'Eat something and then we're going on … without him!'

Him, of course, was Mr Marks, lying still and cold.

Zesh looked at the motionless body, then back to Axel. 'We can't.'

Axel sneered. 'Leave him here, and the next time we stop, I'll give you your inhaler. How about that?'

Zesh would have sold his soul at that moment for his inhaler. He thought about it constantly, imagined it in his hand. He imagined that one magic puff of air blowing into his mouth, travelling down into his lungs, chamber by chamber. When he thought about it like that he could almost feel its magic working, his lungs opening up, until finally, he could breathe again.

But just leave Mr Marks here. Could he do that?

It was as if Axel was reading his mind. 'You've got a choice here, pal. Leave the teacher and breathe or stay here without your inhaler.'

'You're a pig!' Zesh stammered.

How could he be so cruel? How could he give him such a choice? What was he going to do?

It was time to move. Axel pulled Liam to his feet, felt him tremble under his hand.

'I'm scared, Axel.'

Axel was just as afraid, but he wouldn't show it. He was in charge. They were going to do what he wanted and he wanted to move on quickly. This was a bad place. This was where they had lost Angie. It was wet here, and getting wetter. He panned his light around the cavern, catching shadows, watching for what? For anything. Any nightmare to leap out at them.

Yes, he wanted out of here, now.

'Come on, Zesh. On your feet.' His look dared Zesh to argue, but Zesh didn't. He had no breath left. Axel held out the inhaler to him, tantalisingly. 'Thought about it, Zesh, eh? No contest. Next time we stop, you get this. For being a good boy, doing what you're told.' Zesh wasn't so bold now, with no breath in him. He could see the defeat in his face. He wanted this inhaler so badly he would sell his mother to get it.

Zesh hauled himself to his feet, clawing at the wall of rock around him. Axel would have no more trouble from him.

'Funny how all your principles go when you want something bad enough, eh, Zesh? Everybody's got their price.' He laughed, enjoying the moment.

Zesh began to move after him.

'We'll send somebody back for the teacher,' Axel said. And, he thought, if it was too late … too bad.

Zesh didn't look at him. As if his shame was stopping him from looking at him.

Axel turned to Fiona, still curled up on the ground. 'Come on, Fiona. Let's get out of here.' He started moving out of the cavern. She'd soon come after them when she found she was alone in the dark.

It was her yell that stopped him in his tracks, hitting the walls like a torrent. 'NO!'

Axel swung round. Fiona was on her feet. Her face, caught in the beam of his lamp, was the colour of dough.

'I'm not moving,' she said. She looked like a wild child. Her purple hair was standing on end, her eyes rimmed with red. This was a different Fiona from anything he'd seen before.

'What?' He couldn't understand what she meant.

'I said, I'm not zonking coming. Are you deaf? I'm staying here. Angie might find her way back. And if we're not here she'll not know which way to go. She'll be lost. So I'm waiting for her.'

With every sentence she took a step closer, her voice becoming louder till it was almost a scream. She was on the verge of hysteria. That's what it was. Too much had happened. That stupid lassie disappearing the way she had (Axel could hardly think of it himself without breaking out in a sweat – her arms flailing, her mouth opening and closing like a fish). And Fiona had gone down after her. Why had she done that? Hysteria. It was the only answer. To add to his problems there was Zesh without a breath, and Liam shaking so much Axel thought his bones would crack and crumble. And now Fiona.

He was not having it. She was coming and that was all about it.

'You've got to come. We're all moving on. We're getting out of here.'

She swung at him. 'Don't try and give me orders. You've not got my inhaler. I'm not a wimp.' She glared at Liam when she said that. 'I'm staying here. She'll come back. I know she will.'

Axel felt like punching her. 'No she won't. She's dead. She must be. Do you understand? DEAD!'

Fiona slapped her hands over her ears to shut out his words. 'I don't believe it! I don't believe it!'

Liam grabbed his arm. 'Axel, make her come!'

Axel didn't know how to do that. All he knew was they had to get out of here. Why couldn't he make her understand that waiting for Angie was useless?

Zesh stumbled against the wall. He wanted to crawl, anything to ease the pain in his back from trying to breathe. Fiona had surprised him. Amazed him. What did she care about Angie? She'd treated her like dirt. And now, this same Fiona was making him feel ashamed. He'd always looked down his nose at her, and now here she was, doing the right thing. Maybe not the wise thing, but the honourable thing. Refusing to move on without Angie, and him, Zesh, who always thought of himself as superior, had been ready to leave Mr Marks behind because of the promise of a breath of life later.

And could he trust Axel to keep his word? Of course he couldn't. Axel would be more likely to hold the inhaler out to him, and just as he was about to grab for it, throw it into the depths, send it hurtling down a hole so that it tumbled down and down and down. Just like Angie. The thought made his skin tighten, made him catch his pained breath again. He was exhausted trying to breathe, wanted to stop, just for a minute. He slid to the ground again.

He kept his eyes on Axel. The idiot didn't know how to handle Fiona. It was almost funny watching him, listening to him blaming everyone for what was happening, too stupid to realise it was all his fault. Angie had fallen because she had tried to force him to give back the inhaler. She wouldn't have done that if he hadn't taken the inhaler in the first place. And Fiona wouldn't be losing the place if Angie was still here. She'd probably be screaming at Angie instead. Axel couldn't see any of this. Zesh could tell by Axel's puzzled, annoyed expression that he thought everyone was losing it, except him.

Painfully, Zesh tried to speak. His words were only a rasp but he had to say them. 'I'm staying here too.'

CHAPTER 23

'Are you daft!' Axel screamed out at Zesh. 'I'm not giving you the inhaler at all if you stay here! What do you want to stay for?' He didn't wait for an answer. 'The two of you are daft. I'm trying to help you here.'

He actually believes that, Liam was thinking, though at that moment coherent thought wasn't something Liam could do. He couldn't stop himself shaking. Hadn't stopped since Angie had – NO! He couldn't bear to think about that, he kept pushing the picture of her terrified face away from him.

Liam watched Axel, who looked as if he was ready to stamp his foot like a toddler who wasn't getting his way. Axel wanted to be in charge. He had been, until Angie fell. Now Fiona was going against him, and Zesh too. Why Zesh? Liam couldn't understand that. He could come on and get his inhaler or stay here, and Liam knew, and Zesh must know too that Axel wouldn't give it to him now. He'd just have to suffer on, trying to breathe. It sounded sore. He would have felt sorry for anyone else, but not Zesh. So sure of himself. Didn't look so sure of himself now.

Axel ran at Zesh and tried to kick him. Zesh moved his legs away just in time. But he hardly glanced at Axel. He was too exhausted.

Liam tried to listen to the sounds in the caves, but all he could hear was Zesh's laboured breathing.

'Right! Fine! Stay here then. But Liam and me, we're moving. Right, Liam.' He turned and scowled at him, daring him to refuse.

Liam nodded. 'Right, big guy.'

Axel swung back at Fiona. 'Are you coming or what?'

It was as if Fiona had forgotten he was there. Liam had never seen her like this. It frightened him. Too many things about all of them were changing.

Zesh wouldn't change his mind now, either. He would stay.

And him? Liam? If he stayed here with them what chance would he have? None. But with Axel – Axel would find a way out. His sense of direction was brilliant. He'd find the way out. And when we get out, he thought, I'll make sure we send someone back for the rest. He even moved towards them and assured them he would. Zesh didn't answer. Fiona ignored him. Only Mr Marks, his face like wax, seemed to hear him. He murmured uneasily, as if he was having a bad dream.

You're lucky, pal, thought Liam. You're having the bad dream, we're living the nightmare.

'Come on, Liam!' Axel called to him. Liam took one last look at Zesh. 'I will send somebody back, I promise.'

Zesh didn't say anything. He saved his breath for Axel with one word, and one pleading look. 'Please ...'

Didn't he know that was the worst thing you could do with Axel? Plead with him. What better way of letting him know he has you in his power?

'Get on with it, Zesh,' Axel snapped. 'It's only asthma. It's not as if you're going to die or anything.'

Zesh watched as Axel and Liam were swallowed up by the darkness. He heard Axel stumble and swear, saw Liam look back and hover uncertainly before he moved after Axel.

Uncertainly. Still didn't know what to do. Still wasn't sure if the decision he was making was the one that would be the best for him. Zesh thought at that moment he hated Liam more than he hated Axel.

But right then he had no energy to hate anyone. He was so scared. Axel at least didn't seem to be aware that you could die from asthma. People did. That was what was frightening Zesh so much. With every passing minute, closer to death. Shut up! He yelled it to himself. Don't think like that. He thought instead of his mother, the way she'd held tight on to his hand during his last attack, whispering softly to him, words of encouragement, soothing words. He closed his eyes and heard her voice again.

'You will be fine, my son.' He could almost hear her breathing for him, and wished more than anything that she was with him now. Holding his hand, talking to him. Allah, help me, he prayed. But why should Allah listen to him? He'd never usually asked for his help.

Fiona stirred beside him. He heard her draw in a long sob. 'Are we going to die, Zesh?' she asked. Then she tutted. 'What am I asking you for? You know as much as I know. What did you stay for, stupid?'

Her insults made him feel better. That was more like the old Fiona – the one he couldn't stand. Goodness, he'd practically been feeling sorry for her for a while. Weeping for Angie, and he hated to admit this bit, but he'd also admired her. Admired the way she'd gone down into that black hole after Angie – admired the way she'd refused to move on without her. Now, with her angry tone, he felt the old familiar rush of annoyance at her and he liked it.

She twisted herself round and stared at him. In this strange, uncanny light, her eyes were bright as buttons. Black buttons, piercing into him.

'What are you playin' at, Zesh? You could have went on – I'd have stayed here wi' him.' She nodded at Mr Marks's limp body. 'You're not doing anybody any good staying here.'

Zesh drew in as much breath as he could. 'Don't … trust … Axel.'

Fiona got to her feet. 'Tell me about it. I don't trust him either. But I'll get him back, you see if I don't.'

All this talk of getting back at people depressed Zesh. 'You wouldn't have been …' he took another long breath, 'scared here on your own?'

He was sure her eyes welled up with tears. 'Do you think Angie's scared wherever she is? She's not got any company. She might be unconscious. She'll wake up and shout or use her whistle, and if I'm not here there won't be anybody to hear her.'

Zesh took a long time to answer that. 'I thought ... you didn't like her.'

Fiona drew her hand across her nose and didn't answer him. Instead, she bent down by Mr Marks. 'Has anybody given him any water? Thought not.' Didn't wait for any response. Typical Fiona. 'See you Mr Marks, as if you weren't in a bad enough state, they want to dehydrate you as well.'

Zesh smiled. 'Ooh, big words,' he said weakly.

She spun round on him. 'Aye, I do know big words. Know a lot of things. I might not read books, but I watch a lot of telly.' She turned back to Mr Marks, twisted open her bottle of water and held it against his lips. He choked a little, his eyelids flickered, then he was still again.

'I think he's got concussion,' Fiona said wisely. She sat back on her heels. 'It was Angie always made sure he had water,' she said. And though she didn't turn her head to look at Zesh, didn't make a sound, Zesh knew she was crying again.

'See, this has got to be the right way. There's practically a path.' Axel was reassuring himself as much as Liam. Liam aimed his beam at the ground. A path? More like broken rocks and boulders, sent hurtling down over eons, breaking up and coming to rest in this horrible place. It was black all around and sometimes in the darkness Liam could hear sounds, scuttling sounds, like tiny things running in and out of rocks. Ants. Spiders. Rats.

He shouted to Axel to stop himself thinking about it. 'Do you really think you can't die of asthma?'

Axel still forged ahead, called back to him. 'Don't be wet. You die of cancer. Or a heart attack. Zesh is a wimp. Can't get his breath, puts on a big act to get sympathy. Well, he's not getting any from me.'

'An act? Do you think it was an act?'

'Too right. How much do you bet that five minutes after he got that inhaler he'd be right as rain. Magic, eh?'

Liam wasn't so sure. Zesh really hadn't looked well. He wondered how they were doing back there.

He almost bumped into Axel, who'd come to a sudden halt. 'What's wrong?'

'Can't go any further,' Axel shrugged. 'We'll have to go back. Find another way.' He sounded surprised, as if he'd been sure this had been the right way.

Liam swung his beam around the broken black rock of the tunnel.

'Wait a minute, Axel.' He swung the beam again. 'There. Look. There is an opening.' He stepped forwards. There was a gap on the ground, narrow, but definitely another narrow tunnel. Liam bent down so his light shone through. He gasped. It led to another chamber. A vast chamber.

'No, you were right, Axel. This is the way. It's like a U-bend, but it goes up into another big cave.'

'It's too wee. We would never get through there. Well, you would. You're anorexic. But not me.'

Liam remembered something Mr Marks had said about getting through small spaces. How it was usually possible. Put your arms above your head, as if you were going to dive through. He'd said that narrowed you right away. Liam pulled off his rucksack. He was going to try it. He wriggled himself inside. It would be tight for Axel, no doubt about that. But he would make it. In a flat-out crawl, like a worm himself, Liam slid through into the other chamber. It was vast, breathtaking, and best of all, dry. He stood up and called out. His voice echoed high up into the rocks and came rushing back at him again and again. 'Come on, Axel!'

He waited but there was no sign of Axel coming through. He bent down and looked through. All he could see was Axel's feet.

'Axel,' he called, but Axel didn't answer him. He crouched down and laid himself flat and once again crawled back through the tunnel.

Axel's face was like paste. He was swallowing nervously. And a thought came to Liam. 'You're not scared, are you, Axel?'

Axel took a deep breath. For a second Liam thought he was going to hit him. But he only yanked off his rucksack, and threw himself on the ground. He looked into the narrow opening. He said nothing for a moment, then finally, 'Me? Scared of nothing!'

CHAPTER 24

Captain Goldner kicks me hard, sending pain shooting up through my leg. 'Get up. Do as you're told from now on. Next time it will be more than your ear I will shoot at.'

I stumble to my feet, pull a rag from my pocket and hold it to my ear. There is so much blood.

'But, sir, where can we go?'

His answer is to swing a blow against my head, knocking me to the ground again. 'I will find their arsenal. I will destroy it. Destroy them.'

He is losing his mind. He must be. If the enemy had weapons stored here, there would be guards, soldiers.

Then, as I trudge behind him, a terrifying thought comes into my mind.

Who needs soldiers when you have an even more fearsome guardian?

* * *

The only sound in the cave was Zesh's breathing. It rasped around the walls like the breath of an old dying man.

It was really getting on Fiona's nerves.

'Can you not stop that for a minute?' she snapped at him. She was trying hard to listen for Angie's voice, sure every second she could hear her calling, and then Zesh's hoarse breathing would smother any other noise.

Zesh looked at her and smiled. 'You're something else, Fiona.'

She watched him as the words struggled out of him. 'Could you really die?'

Zesh didn't speak. He just nodded.

'I kinda thought that,' she said. 'I saw this programme about it on telly. Some film star died of it, you know.'

'Thank you for that,' Zesh croaked.

Fiona turned her eyes on the teacher. 'Do you think he'll die?' she asked.

Zesh rolled his eyes. 'You're a ... barrel of laughs, Fiona.'

That took so much out of him. He leaned back, exhausted. Fiona ignored him. She was thinking now of Angie. 'I don't think she's dead. I really don't.' She was almost talking to herself. Yet she was glad that Zesh, someone, was there in the dark listening. 'I think she's somewhere, unconscious, and when she comes to she'll climb back up here.' Angie climbing anywhere seemed improbable. 'Or she'll shout.' That sounded more likely. 'Aye, she'll shout.'

Fiona felt her throat tighten. 'I was so horrible to her. D'you know that? I called her fat and ugly. I thought she was a wimp. Always going on about being a Girl Guide, always that cheery, always looking on the bright side. She got right up my nose.' She looked at Zesh. 'I'm a horrible person, so I am?'

Zesh said nothing, but she didn't need an answer. She knew what she was.

'She wanted us both to jump Axel. Did you know that? She thought her and I could take him, force him to give you back the inhaler. And d'you know what I said? I said, Don't be so stupid, Angie. But she wasn't stupid, was she? She was brave. I think I'm so smart and she was the stupid one. But she was the one that was ready to jump Axel.'

She covered her face with her hands, blotting out the picture of Angie falling …

'I'll never forgive myself for that, Zesh. See from

now on, I'm going to be a better person. For Angie's sake. I'm going to try harder for her sake as well. I'll even help Mr Marks, there ye are!'

Zesh still didn't say a word. Too breathless. But his eyes said he didn't believe her.

'The leopard cannot change its spots, is that what you're thinking? Typical Zesh, never look on the good side of me. Well, I'll show you. Anyway, where do you get off criticising me! You were going to leave Marks here so you could get your inhaler. So you're every bit as bad as I am.'

She dared him to disagree with her, but still he said nothing. 'OK, I know, you could die without that inhaler. I didn't know that before. And do you know what? I don't think Axel knows it either. I mean, he's thick. You should have told him. I don't think he's that bad. He wouldn't have kept your inhaler off you if he knew you might die.' Zesh stared at her.

'Aye, you're right. He is that bad,' she said after a moment. She leaned back against the wall. 'It's good having somebody to talk to, ain't it?' Zesh let out a long sigh. She was sure he was disagreeing with her. 'Mind you, you're even annoying when you're quiet.'

* * *

'I can't move,' Axel said again, and Liam answered again, 'Sure you can.'

Liam sounded annoyed. Axel should be angry with him about that. He should be lashing out at him, so he knew who was the boss. But all he could think of was … he could not move. He wanted to try to sidle back. He was here in the middle of this black hole and he couldn't go back, go forwards, go anywhere.

Yet, he couldn't let the likes of Liam see his fear.

And what was there to be scared of? He wasn't scared of the dark. The rest of them were. But not him. The dark held no fears for him

He wasn't scared of any creepy crawlies that might emerge out of the rock. He wasn't even scared of the Worm. A legend. A made-up story to frighten children.

There were too many real life-terrors to be feared.

The ground beneath him was hard and damp. He felt as if he was clamped in rock. Like being in a coffin. And it was as if a memory deep in his subconscious was burrowing to the surface. He gasped with fear and Liam touched his leg. 'I'll try pushing you.'

Axel could just see the other chamber, inches away, an eternity away. It looked dry and wide. He could stand up in there, stretch and jump. He longed to be there, but he couldn't move. He was so tight in the rock he couldn't even shake with fear. He tried to move an inch forwards, felt the rock scraping against his face. I'll get through it, he kept saying to himself. I'll be fine.

He felt as if the rock didn't want to let him go, as if it was an enemy. Getting back at him for Angie, for letting her fall, for not going after her. Or avenging Zesh, who was lying desperately trying to breathe on the cold damp floor of another cave.

NO!

Had he shouted it aloud? He didn't think so. All he knew for certain was that he had never been more afraid.

Yes you have, the memory seemed to whisper to him. A memory he had always locked away.

'Relax, breathe in ... squeeze yourself through.' Liam's words were trying to reassure him, but nothing would. Axel closed his eyes. He couldn't bear the thought of the rock so close to his face, pressing down on him, rock above him, rock all around him. No escape.

His eyes snapped open. He didn't mean them to, they just did. And it was like a black stony face staring down at him, touching him. Immovable. Maybe this had been a man once, just like him, squeezing through, finding himself stuck for ever.

Turned into stone.

Merging into rock.

No! He had to get out of here. It suddenly didn't matter to him if Liam did know how frightened he was. He yelled. 'NO!' Began to struggle wildly to free himself.

Real mind-bending terror set in then. He couldn't move. Not back. Not forwards. Stuck. His nightmare. His memory … the jaws of it opened up and sucked him in.

A little boy, locked in a tiny trunk for being bad, screaming to get out, pounding on the lid. Told he would never be let out. Believing it.

'NO!' He yelled it again and his terrified scream echoed through the cavern. Over and over he yelled. 'NO!'

Liam was trying frantically to pull him back. 'I'll get you. I will.' He tried to put his hand between Axel and the rock, but there was no space. 'You can't be stuck. You can't be.' But he didn't sound so sure now.

This was Axel's worst nightmare. The worst he could ever imagine. Here in the dark, pressed against solid rock, for ever.

And Axel screamed so loud a tremor went through the cave.

CHAPTER 25

'What was that noise, Zesh?' Fiona was on her feet the instant she heard it. A scream. Was it a scream? It seemed to wail through the caves like a train in a tunnel. 'This place gives me the creeps.' She waited for another scream, but the sound died away till all she could hear was Zesh, struggling to breathe.

She sat down again. 'Did it sound like a girl's scream?' She looked at Zesh. 'It did, didn't it?' She wanted him to tell her that it couldn't have been Angie. Not screaming like that. There was so much terror in that sound. It probably wasn't even a scream, she decided. 'There's so many weird noises in here, isn't there?' She shivered. It was getting colder. Why was that? Were they closer to the sea? 'It's never quiet.'

There were sounds, that swished through the tunnels and whooshed and whispered. Sounds you could never quite catch. Sounds you heard but when you stopped to listen they would swish past your ear and down into another cave.

And Angie was somewhere on her own, listening to those same sounds.

If she could listen to anything.

Fiona scrubbed that thought from her mind. She wouldn't think like that. She'd think like Angie. Always looking on the bright side. She'd find her.

The only sound now was from Zesh, and it was getting on her wick.

Mr Marks was better company than he was. She turned her beam on Zesh and he blinked weakly. 'Is it really that bad?'

He couldn't even answer that. 'You look awful, Zesh. You're always that smart. You always look as if your mother had ironed your uniform with you still in it. You get on everybody's zonking nerves. I always look like an unmade bed – mind you, did an unmade bed not win some big prize?' She thought about that. 'Saw that on television. So there you are, I'm a work of art really.' She grinned at him. Zesh was too weak even to grin back.

'I'm trying to cheer you up here. You could at least be zonking grateful.'

To her complete and utter surprise Zesh said, very softly, 'Sorry.'

'What! Did you just apologise? I wish I had a tape recorder. Zesh apologises. That must be a first for you. There must be two moons in the sky.' Fiona sighed then. 'I wish I could see the sky to check.' She fumbled in her bag for water. 'Do you want some of this? I'm going to give some to Marks.'

This time Zesh nodded and Fiona held the bottle to the teacher's lips first. The water trickled in and his lips moved to catch it. At least he was still alive.

Then she turned to Zesh. And handed him the bottle. It looked like a struggle for him even to lift it to his lips.

Fiona watched him thoughtfully. 'You know, Zesh, I saw this programme on television. It was about asthma. Some new breathing technique ...' She paused, thinking. 'People that breathe like that don't even need an inhaler.'

She saw Zesh's eyes grow bright with hope. Was that hope? It looked like it. 'I wish I could remember what it was. It'll come to me.' She closed her eyes, thinking hard. Once she clicked into that programme, maybe she could help Zesh to breathe.

* * *

Liam tried to calm Axel down. He'd never seen Axel like this. He was terrified. Liam was sure he was crying.

'Hold still. I'm trying to push you through.'

But Axel wasn't listening. He was trying desperately to free himself and only seemed to be clamping himself further into his rock prison.

'Get me out of here. Get me out of here. Get me out of here.' He repeated it over and over like a prayer. Liam couldn't see his face, but he could picture him staring at rock, unable to turn his head this way or that. Liam was working frantically, trying to clear rock beneath Axel, trying to make more room so he could push him gently through. Mr Marks had said, you had to be calm in tight corners. Well, they didn't come much tighter than this. But how could he get Axel to be calm?

Liam felt a shiver run through Axel's body, a shiver of fear. Why had they come this way! Because it was the only way, he reminded himself. It was the right way. It had to be. Don't scream again, Axel, he prayed. Because that scream of his had cut through him like steel through bone. It was the scream of someone in terror, or someone confronted with their worst nightmare.

Liam sat back on his heels, exhausted.

'Don't stop! Don't stop.' Axel was almost pleading. He was struggling to breathe. He sounded at that moment just like Zesh had. Was Axel thinking the same thing?

Liam didn't believe Axel was thinking at all. Instinct had taken over, the instinct to survive. Suddenly, he cried out so loudly that Liam jerked back. 'Get me out of here!'

But he'd never get him out while he was panicking like that. 'Listen to me, Axel. Listen.' Now Liam's voice was forceful. It didn't sound like him at all. It took him by surprise. It surprised Axel into silence. 'I'm going to get you through there, but you have to do what I say. You have to do what I say.'

Axel swore at him. Liam swore back. And then Axel said nothing. He listened. Liam probed through his memory for everything Marks had told them about calmness, teamwork. 'I want you to take deep breaths, Axel. Breathe in. Breathe out.'

Axel yelled again. 'Are you stupid!'

'You'll get through this if you do what I say.' He could imagine Axel making a supreme effort, but he couldn't manage it. His breath was still coming in gasps.

'I'm never getting out of here, am I? I'm going to be

stuck here, for ever and ever.' He began to roar and push and Liam knew if he couldn't stop him now he might just be stuck there for ever. He felt like screaming too, but that wasn't going to help anybody. He gripped Axel's ankles.

'Close your eyes, Axel. Don't think about anything, except breathing. In through your nose, out through your mouth. Slowly, Axel, slowly. In. Out.'

He heard a sound and it took him a minute to realise what it was. Axel's teeth were chattering.

'Liam, I'm shit scared,' Axel stuttered.

'That's right, Zesh, in through your nose, out through your mouth.'

For ten minutes Fiona had been talking Zesh through this breathing technique. Breathing less deeply but still fully from the abdomen. She'd seen them doing it on television. Was it helping? He couldn't be sure. Maybe a little.

She breathed along with him, in and out, nattering on relentlessly about this programme and that. Was that all she did, watch television? Zesh was glad she had. In spite of everything she was making him laugh. Maybe it was way deep down, but she was definitely making him laugh. She talked such a load of rubbish.

And yet ...

In. Out. He did feel slightly, ever so slightly better. The pain in his chest, in his back, was just as bad but the breathing, did that seem easier? Please let it be.

Positive thinking.

It *was* helping. It *was* getting easier.

He wanted to talk to her, but for the moment, he had no energy.

'Do you think Axel and Liam are OK?' Fiona asked. 'I know what you're thinking, who cares? But if they don't get out of here, how will we? Maybe they're out already.' She strained her ears to listen for the sound of rescue, but all Zesh could hear were the strange sounds that seemed to crawl through the caves like something alive.

'Do you think that scream could have been Liam?' Fiona seemed to dismiss that right away with a toss of her head. 'It wasn't even a scream, it was just a noise. These caves are full of noises.' And once again she seemed to strain to listen.

Liam's hands were bleeding as he clawed at the rock beneath Axel. Axel was silent as stone, breathing deeply just as Liam had instructed him. Too terrified to move, except for the tremors that seemed to pass through his body, as if he himself was rock and earthquakes raged deep inside him.

He could hear the trickle of water behind him. The cave, it seemed to him, was getting wetter. He kept asking, 'All right, Axel?' but there was no answer.

'We're getting there, I promise.' This was the only remark that drew a response. Axel let out a low moan. Almost like a prayer.

Liam felt him relax and in that second he pushed Axel as hard as he could. He felt him move, Axel felt it too, for he came alive in that second and began to edge himself through.

'Careful now,' Liam said softly 'Calmly does it. You're getting there.'

Inch by inch Axel moved forwards. He was almost there. He would get out! The joy of freedom came out of Axel in a roar. Liam heard it and knew he was through.

Liam scrabbled through after him. It was nothing for him. His hands ached and bled. The two boys stood looking at each other. Axel's face was strained with the fear still. He looked at Liam for a long time, then he said softly, 'Thanks, Liam.'

Liam collapsed to the ground, exhausted. In that moment he knew something had changed for ever.

CHAPTER 26

'Did you hear that?' Liam stood up and looked around, his headlamp sending an eerie beam through the chamber.

Axel watched him warily. His head was splitting with the pain throbbing in his temples. He took off his helmet and lay back, more exhausted than he'd ever felt in his life.

Liam looked down at him. 'You OK, big guy?'

Axel couldn't meet his gaze. Liam had seen him afraid – more than afraid – terrified. Had he cried? He couldn't remember, didn't want to go back, even in his mind, to that awful time. Those hours – or was it only minutes? – that he'd been trapped … NO! Don't go there again.

'Say something, Axel.' Liam sounded as if he was worried. Axel's mouth was too dry with fear to say a word. Instead he gave the thumbs-up sign.

Liam crouched down and his light beaming into Axel's eyes made him throw his hand up to shield them.

'Sorry,' Liam said, and he turned his lamp away from Axel's face. 'I've never seen you like that. You were really scared.'

Any other time Axel would have punched him for even suggesting that. But now, he couldn't even look into Liam's face. Liam said nothing for a long while. When he did speak he took Axel by surprise. 'Give me Zesh's inhaler.' He held out his hand.

Now Axel did look at him, and he felt he was seeing Liam for the first time. His long thin face, his weak mouth. Yet now, his eyes were bright and bold in the half-light from his lamp.

'So, this is your game.' Axel found his voice finally. 'Now you want to be in charge, is that it?'

Liam beckoned with his hand. 'Gimme it.'

Axel thought about refusing. He could beat Liam with one hand tied behind his back. But what would be the use? Liam knew the truth. He was a coward. He'd cried. Now he would tell everyone about that. He fumbled inside his pocket, took it out. Thought for a second about throwing it away, maybe it would disappear down a hole, just like –

He caught his breath even thinking about that. It sent a chill, like a tongue of ice, down his back. Angie, somewhere, maybe stuck like him?

He handed Liam the inhaler. It didn't matter now. Nothing mattered now.

'I'm staying here,' he said. 'I'm not going on. Send somebody back for me if you want, I don't care. I'm not moving.'

Liam took the inhaler and looked at it. 'We've got to go back for them, Axel.'

Axel's eyes went wide with alarm. 'Are you kidding! No!'

'The water, Axel. The water's rising. It's gonny flood the caves. We've got to bring them here. Or they'll all drown.'

Axel thought about it. The ice-cold water rising, Zesh and Fiona and Marks, all trapped. Didn't make any difference. 'I'm not going back.'

'I need you to help, Axel, help with the teacher.'

Axel would have cried but he stopped himself. 'No. I canny go back through there. Liam, don't ask me. Please, Liam.'

He was begging him. Begging Liam? It seemed to Axel that he'd never noticed how tall Liam was. 'You go back. Give Zesh his inhaler. Then he'll be able to help you.' Axel turned his face to the wall. 'Don't ask me to go back there.'

'I think that's working, Zeshie old boy!' Fiona patted him on the back. 'Here, maybe I should become a nurse. No, scrap that. A doctor. Dr Fiona Duncan.' She was off in her own little world again. 'I watch that *ER* all the time. I could probably amputate somebody's leg with my eyes shut.'

And Zesh laughed. He actually laughed. The first time he'd been able to do anything but try to breathe for so long.

'Maybe if you keep getting better you could move on. Not me, of course. I'm waiting for Angie, but you could move.'

'Worried about me?' Zesh smiled.

'No. I want rid of you.' But she smiled too.

'Thanks, Fiona,' he said.

Fiona pretended to faint. 'First an apology, and now a thanks! There must be two moons in the sky.' She took a long breath. 'I would do anything to see the moon again, Zesh. What would you like to see?'

Zesh thought about that. The sun, the flowers, but

there was only one thing, one person he wanted to see.

'My mum,' he said. He thought about how often he'd ignored her, always listening to his dad – never taking her advice, unless it was his dad's advice too. Didn't care if she turned up at parents' nights, just as long as his dad was there.

Now, he wanted to see her smiling at him again, wanted to feel her cool fingers stroke his face, wanted so much to hear her voice.

'I wonder what my mum's doing now?' Fiona thought aloud. 'She'll either be at the bingo, or she has booked up a cheap holiday in Benidorm with her galpals while I'm away. You know, when I'm old and decrepit, I want to be like my mother.'

Zesh laughed again. 'She'd kill you if she heard you say that.'

There was a sudden noise in the cave, a beam of light channelling towards them. Fiona leaped to her feet. 'Angie!' she shouted. 'I knew she'd come back.'

But it wasn't Angie. It was Liam.

Liam had heard them talking, even heard Zesh laughing. That had really surprised him. He'd expected, as he pushed his way back to them, that he would find Zesh as unconscious as Mr Marks, and Fiona still crying or off in search of Angie.

Instead, they were laughing.

'How come you're back?' Fiona asked. 'Axel go on without you?'

Liam stayed silent. He had it all in his power now. Zesh's inhaler in his pocket. Axel's secret locked inside him. It was all he'd ever wanted – to be the one in control – and now here it all was, his for the taking.

'Where is Axel?' Zesh's voice was still weak, his breath still came in gasps. But he was still breathing.

Liam made his decision. Maybe he had never doubted for a moment what that decision would be.

'Axel's waiting for us. We found a big cave. A dry cave. It's got to lead to the sea.'

'Axel's waiting?' Fiona sounded as if she could not believe that. 'Sure he's not just run off and left you?'

'Come on, the water's rising. This cave will be filled up soon. It happens fast. We've got to go.'

Zesh shook his head. 'I can't.'

Liam bent down to him and placed the inhaler in his hands. 'Yes you can, Zesh. Here.'

'How did you get that from Axel?'

Liam shrugged his shoulders. 'I got it. OK?'

Fiona pushed at his shoulder. 'And what about Angie? I'm not just going to go off and leave her.'

Liam wanted to shout at her, but he didn't. His voice was calm. 'You've got no choice now!' he said. She wasn't ever coming back, but he couldn't bear to think that either. 'This cave is flooding. We'll find Angie somewhere else. We'll send people back for her. But the sooner we get out of here, the quicker we can do that.'

'He's right,' Zesh said, gripping the inhaler as if it was a winning lottery ticket, or pure gold. Then he lifted it to his mouth, and breathed in.

CHAPTER 27

Axel wasn't afraid. Not of being alone in the dark. It was strange, that. One beam of light from his helmet was all that split the darkness. Yet he didn't fear anything, on either side of him, or above him, or behind him. He feared nothing. He had faced his worst fear. A fear he didn't even realise he had, and now, nothing else mattered.

He wondered idly if Liam would come back for him, and realised that didn't matter now either. If he had to stay here, he would. He didn't care. He pulled his rucksack towards him and opened it. He hadn't taken water, though the teacher had told them to. He had ignored that and had taken Coke instead. He unscrewed the top and slugged it down. When it was done, he'd drink water. There would be plenty of water soon, if Liam was right.

Liam.

Was he even now telling Zesh and Fiona how Axel had cried? How he'd been like a stuck pig? Was that the sound he could hear now trickling through the caves?

Were they all laughing, laughing at him?

The Coke was making him feel better, stronger – and angrier.

The likes of Liam laughing at him? He'd get him for that.

Of course, he couldn't get him if Liam never came back. Maybe they'd never be found. Maybe they'd become a part of the legend that surrounded these caves. Like the cannibal family, like the Nazis. Like the Worm.

Did any of them frighten him now? If he met a cannibal family he'd eat them. That's how hungry he was. And the Nazis. They'd be long dead.

But the Worm?

Axel listened again. What strange sounds in these caves. How could people climb down here and actually enjoy it? Then he remembered weirdo Marks. He enjoyed it. This was his world, he had once told them. And Axel remembered now how sinister it had sounded to him then.

Well, they were in another world now.

And he was alone.

*   *   *

Zesh couldn't believe how much better he felt. Exhausted, yes, and his back still ached with the pressure of trying to breathe, but here he was pulling, lifting Mr Marks along with Fiona and Liam. How could he explain to anyone how happy he felt?

Even Fiona's moaning was making him feel happy.

'I should never have left there. I'm too easily led, that's my problem. Liam just has to say, "Move, Fiona, we're goin' to drown, if we stay here" and I just say, "OK, Liam, you're the boss."'

Liam, struggling with the teacher, shook his head. 'You, easily led? Come on, Fiona. Anyway, you know we had to move. You can see the water's rising.'

He was right. The water was running down the cave walls, running in channels along the cave floor. The sounds of it were everywhere. Zesh felt as if a river of water was ready to burst into the cavern.

Yet, it was puzzling. Liam, and right. Two words that just didn't seem to go together. Liam, telling them what to do. Liam, in charge. Zesh had been sure he would have another argument on his hands when he insisted on taking Mr Marks with him. Instead, Liam had almost suggested it before Zesh had.

'If you're feeling OK now, Zesh, you can help us with the teacher.'

And Fiona had moaned. 'I've got to help? Me? A weak wee female? Carry a big lump like him?'

That had made both him and Liam laugh. Fiona, a weak wee female!

She carried Mr Marks along with them, though it was always a struggle. She was surprising Zesh. No. He was surprising himself. Because he found that he liked her. He liked the way she was determined to stay and wait for Angie. He liked the way she didn't panic. And he liked, especially, the way she'd helped him.

They were following the marks that Axel had made against the rock. 'Are we nearly there, Liam?' Zesh asked.

Liam stopped, breathing hard. He laid down the teacher. 'Let's rest for a minute,' he said, then he answered. 'We're close.'

'You're sure? All these tunnels look the same.' Fiona said. 'Are these the only ones you marked?'

'This is the only one you can stand upright in. Axel and I tried them all. Honest. This is the way we came. I promise.' Liam said it with assurance, and took his whistle and blew into it. The sound seemed to carry through the black tunnels. They all waited for the answering whistle, but no sound came back to them.

'So where's Axel?'

And Liam didn't know how to answer her.

Zesh sat back, glad of the rest. 'Why didn't Axel come back with you?'

Liam didn't look at him, and he took a long time in answering. As if he was considering his answer. 'He's back there, waiting for us.'

Zesh felt sure he was lying. He was protecting Axel. Typical Liam. And yet, here he needn't be afraid of Axel. So, was there another reason he was lying? With Liam you just couldn't be sure.

Zesh lay against the rock and closed his eyes. You didn't recover from an asthma attack in a moment. It would take a long while. He prayed it was over. That his breath was slowly coming back to normal. All he wanted to do now, was sleep.

Axel slept too. Dreams of long dark tunnels and strange noises and people laughing. He was sure he could hear people laughing. Their laughter mocking him from cave to cave to cave. Someone was calling him. He could hear them through his dream.

'Axel,' they called. 'Axel, we need you.'

But even in his dream, he thought, no one needs me. No one needs Axel O'Rourke.

So he didn't listen.

But the voice kept calling him through his dream. 'Axel. Axel. Help us, Axel.'

Still, he wouldn't listen. It was a dream, and he didn't want to wake up from it.

'I told you he'd just up and leave whenever he got the chance!' Fiona said. 'He'd never wait for us.'

They were at the crack in the rock where Liam and Axel had pushed their way through. They could hear water gushing close by. Liam was sure they had better get into that other chamber as soon as possible. But where was Axel?

Liam shouted for him again. He blew his whistle.

'You're sure you're at the right place?' Zesh asked him. 'It looks so much like a dead end.'

Liam flashed his light against the narrow opening. Fiona shook her head in disbelief as she had when she'd first seen it. 'You're not trying to tell me that Axel, big Axel, got through that!' She got to her knees and peered through. 'I'd like to have seen that.'

No, you wouldn't, Fiona, Liam thought. He went cold even remembering it. Axel stuck in that tight narrow passage, crying, scared. And he'd been as scared as Axel. Not knowing what to do to help him, and yet, he had helped him, he'd got him through.

'Axel!' he yelled again.

They were all still for a second, listening. But there was no answering whistle. No shout. 'We don't need him,' Zesh said. 'We can get through without him. We can get Mr Marks through.'

'Can we?' Fiona looked from the teacher's still bulk to the narrow passage and let out a cry. 'I don't think so!'

'At least he's relaxed. He said you've got to be relaxed to get through crawlspaces like this,' Liam said.

Fiona let out a laugh. 'Well, you don't get much more relaxed than him.'

'You've remembered everything Mr Marks told us, Liam.' Zesh sounded so surprised it angered Liam.

'You think I'm too stupid to remember anything!'

Zesh began to apologise. 'No. I didn't mean it like that.'

'Och, shut up about who remembers what! Get moving.'

Liam crouched down, and lowered himself into the opening. 'I'll go through first. Gimme the rucksacks, then I can help pull through Mr Marks.'

He began to crawl through to the other side, pulling the rucksacks behind him. Once he was through he flung the bags on the flat ground, then he bent back under the hole and called to Zesh, 'Pass him through head first.'

'Right, Liam.'

It amazed him that the likes of Zesh was doing as he asked. He gripped the teacher's shoulders and tried to pull. This was going to be tight. Almost as tight as it had been with Axel. But he had managed to clear some loose rock, so surely it should be easier this time?

'Clear some more of the rock back there,' Liam called to Zesh, doing the same on his side. He winced with pain as the raw wounds on his hands opened up again. The teacher could have been dead he was so still. If he opened his eyes now, he would see only rock. He wouldn't be able to turn his head. What if he reacted the way Axel had?

Don't think of that, Liam told himself. Once we get Mr Marks clear we can all get into the big chamber, safe from the rising water, on our way home. Surely they must find a way out from there.

Zesh's voice dashed his hopes. 'It's no use, Liam.' There was still a breathlessness in his voice. He hadn't the strength. Liam gripped the teacher's shoulders tighter, but he was skinny. A runt. He had even less strength than Zesh.

They needed Axel. Axel was strong.

'Axel!!!!!' He screamed out his name. This time he had to come.

CHAPTER 28

It wasn't a dream. Axel realised that now. It was Liam's voice calling him. He sat up, shone his light around the cave, and couldn't see him.

'Where are you?' He knew the answer almost as soon as he asked the question. He was … in there. In that tight, dark tunnel.

'You have to come and help us.' Liam's voice gasped with exhaustion.

Axel jumped to his feet, and stepped back, almost as if some unseen fist had reached out to grab him. He was shaking his head. Back, in there? No chance.

'Are you stuck?'

'Not me, Axel.' His voice had that eerie echoing quality. Ghostly. Was this really Liam? he thought. Or was it his ghost, luring him back into his worst nightmare? Like … like … he tried to remember the name of the women who used their ghostly voices to lure sailors on to rocks.

Sirens. They were called sirens.

'Axel!' Liam shouted. 'It's Mr Marks. I can't pull him through by myself. You've got to help.'

Without a second's hesitation Axel shouted back, 'Leave him.'

'I can't leave him, Axel. And anyway, Zesh and Fiona are on the other side They've got to get through as well.'

Zesh and Fiona. What did he care about them? 'Leave him,' he said again. 'He's caused us nothing but trouble.'

'Axel …' Liam called again.

I wish I could see him, Axel thought. It's scary knowing he's there, calling out to me and I can't see him.

'Please, Axel, hurry, the water's rising on the other side.'

Why should he help anybody? None of them liked him, and as for Marks, why should he do anything to help *him*? This was all his fault.

'Axel! Are you there?'

Axel could hear him, but he couldn't answer him. He even switched off his lamp. If Liam thought he wasn't there, that he'd moved on ahead, he would stop calling to him. Maybe.

No one could expect him to go back into that tunnel. The death dream picture of that rock wall suffocating him made him catch his breath, as if he was still there. Still trapped. No. Nothing would make him go back down into that hole that only worms should inhabit.

'Don't ask me to go back,' he heard himself say. 'Cannae do it.'

'Please,' Liam called to him.

Was that a scream he could hear in the distance? A yell that could only come from Fiona. Screaming at him to come. No use. He wasn't going. The terror of that memory hung about him, whispering in his ear that if he went back down there, it would never let him out this time. He would be trapped down there for ever, merging into rock, becoming stone. He felt once again the stone wrapping itself around him. Felt it touching his face, so he couldn't move his head in any direction. Not ever again.

Marks was in there now. Trapped like him. Axel's bones turned to ice.

No. No one could expect him to go back there.

Liam waited for an age. Finally, he gave up. There was no point wasting energy by shouting again. Axel wasn't coming. 'We'll just have to keep trying to get him out by ourselves.'

Fiona screamed. 'That's what we've been trying to do, stupid. Axel was right. We should have left him.'

Liam thought that even Mr Marks would have said the same thing. They should have left him behind.

'Now me and Zesh are stuck back here ... and the water's coming in here fast.'

Fiona's voice trembled. She'd never admit to being frightened, but she sounded scared.

Liam pulled again at Mr Marks, hoping he would find a strength he never knew he had. People did that. He'd read about mothers lifting cars from their children, of people showing superhuman strength when they most needed it. He gripped the teacher's shoulders, and he prayed. Sweat broke from him, ran down his face. He tried with everything he had left to pull the teacher through, knowing that Zesh and Fiona were doing the same on the other side of the hole.

'Can't do it,' he said, almost to himself.

'It's no use,' Zesh called through the rock.

He knew it was useless. Skinny Liam, how could he hope to have the strength to haul at the teacher, pull him to safety?

In that one moment of despair, he was pulled by the legs right out of the hole. 'I'll get him.' It was Axel. He knocked Liam out of the way. He didn't even look at him. His eyes focused on the teacher, nothing else. As if he was trying to shut out where he was, with the walls closing in on him.

Liam shouted with excitement. 'Axel's here!'

'Axel!' He heard the shock in Fiona's voice.

Liam touched Axel's shoulder. 'What made you –'

'– change my mind?' Axel finished for him. Still he didn't look at him. 'Couldn't let even him be stuck here for ever. Not here.'

He slid himself down back into that tiny space. It was then that Liam saw just how strong Axel really was, as he pulled the teacher through the narrow opening, inch by inch. Concentrating hard, Liam was sure, because he needed to forget where he was.

'We're doing it!' Liam yelled back to Zesh and Fiona. And when they heard him they started yelling. 'Hurry up!'

Lifting him up the U-bend was the hardest part. Liam could never have done that alone. Axel was needed for that. He backed out of the hole, hauling Mr Marks by the shoulders. And behind the teacher Fiona scrabbled through. Zesh followed her, twisting himself through, looking unkempt and sweaty. Together they hauled the teacher up on to the high ground in the chamber and laid him flat.

Only then did Axel fall back, drained. Liam was shaking. Fiona was trying to stop the tears. Zesh lay flat, took out his inhaler and breathed in again. Deep in the other chamber they could hear the rush of water filling it up. As if it was flooding already. They had made it just in time.

'We've probably killed him, dragging him through there.' Fiona was moaning again, feeling for a pulse. She threw the teacher's limp hand from her. 'What am I doing? I'm no zonking Florence Nightingale. I don't even know where a pulse is.'

They had slept after their ordeal, for how long, none of them knew. But now, they were all wondering why Mr Marks had hardly stirred. Was he dying? He looked as if he was. 'Maybe we broke something. I mean, how does he no' wake up?'

'You said it was concussion. Remember? You were going to be a doctor earlier,' Zesh reminded Fiona.

'Trust you to remember that!' she snapped at him.

'We've taken him this far, we might as well take him the rest.' It was Liam who said it and no one argued. Not even Axel. 'We must be close. The caves lead out to the Doon,' he said.

Fiona looked at him in surprise. 'You really did listen to him, didn't you?'

'Course I did,' Liam said. 'The chamber's bigger here. We follow this and it has to lead us out to the sea.'

They didn't say that Mr Marks had also said not all the caves led out to the sea: under the island there was a warren of caves, some of them leading nowhere.

Fiona grinned at him. 'Quite a wee bossy boots when you put your mind to it, eh Liam?'

Liam wanted to smile back, but he didn't dare. What if Zesh laughed at him, or Axel?

Fiona turned to Axel. 'That was great by the way, Axel. We really needed you there.'

Axel stared at her, as if he was expecting one of her smart remarks. She wanted to reassure him that she meant every word. 'I'm serious. Not that you shouldn't have helped us anyway. We needed a big strong boy, and that's you.'

Zesh added softly, almost as if he was forcing the words out. 'Yes, thanks, Axel.'

That really got up Fiona's nose. 'What are you thanking him for? He took your inhaler. That was one crap thing to do.'

'He made up for it,' Zesh said.

That only made her worse. 'Made up for it! He didn't even come back to get you. Liam probably only got it because it fell out of Axel's pocket and he never noticed. He wouldn't spit on you if you were on fire. So less of the *Friends* patter. You'll be wanting a group hug next. One good deed does not make a hero!'

'Shut up, Fiona!' they all shouted.

They didn't know, Axel was thinking. Liam hadn't told them that Axel had handed the inhaler back meekly. Why? He couldn't bear to look at Liam, because he didn't know how he felt about that. Why hadn't he told them? Was it because he wanted to wait until Axel was with them, and then humiliate him? And yet, here he was, and Liam still hadn't said a word. He wanted to ask him why. In fact, he wanted to grab Liam, push him up against a wall, make him tell just what his game was.

But that kind of behaviour seemed an age away. He could never treat Liam like that again. Maybe he'd never be able to treat anyone like that again.

Axel glanced at Zesh, lying back against the wall. He held tightly on to that inhaler of his. He'd never let it out of his hand again. And would Axel do what he had done before? Attack him, run at him, take it from him?

No. That was in another life, another world. The world up there. Down here, they had all changed.

Liam stood up. 'Time we were moving,' he said.

And they all stood up and followed him.

CHAPTER 29

There was a spring in their step as they moved forwards now. Zesh supposed the rest of them felt as he did – they were on their way out. They had to be. They had all faced the worst and come through it.

All except Angie. His heart sank when he thought of poor Angie and her fate. He glanced at Fiona, on the other side of Mr Marks. Had she forgotten already? Somehow he didn't think she had.

She caught him watching her. 'What are you looking at!' she demanded. She didn't expect an answer. 'I don't even think he's as heavy as he was.' She meant Mr Marks. 'Do you think he's lost weight?'

But of course, Axel was now taking a lot of the teacher's weight. Axel was strong. Zesh had been so sure he would have objected to taking the teacher on with them, but no. When Liam had told him to lift him, he had lifted him. Maybe now that Axel had actually saved

Mr Marks's life, he felt responsible for him. Whatever the reason, it was a big change. Axel had changed. So had Liam. Had he, Zesh, changed? All he knew was that he was happy to move along behind Liam, finding his breathing easier with every passing moment.

'If Angie was here she would have us singing.' He regretted mentioning Angie right away.

Fiona let out a cry. 'Don't talk about Angie. I left her. Maybe she came back.'

But they all knew now, that even if she had come back, she would be doomed. Drowned in the black water that filled the caves behind them. Fiona stopped suddenly. 'I was so nasty to her, and she never even noticed. She was always telling stories and I never believed her. She never took offence, no matter how nasty you were to her.'

'You were nicer to her than the rest of us,' Zesh said.

'Aye, I suppose I was.' A moment later she was off again. 'She was a really nice person. See Angie, what you saw was what you got. No secrets. She was just Angie.'

Zesh had to agree with that. Angie had been a nice girl when they'd come on the trip, and with the last thing she'd done, trying to help Zesh, she was still a nice girl. 'It's funny though,' he said. 'We never really knew anything about her. Where she came from, or anything. We'll never know now. Now that she's …'

Axel burst into the conversation. 'I suppose that's my fault.' He'd hardly spoken before this, and his voice seemed to boom out through the caves. 'Suppose it was. But I didn't push her. You can all swear to that. I never touched her.'

Did he think they were going to blame him?

'Time enough to talk about Angie when we get out,' Liam said. 'Let's get on.'

There was a feeling, Zesh was sure they all felt it, that there was a need for speed. No stopping, maybe a final rush to the outside world. They moved on silently, but each thinking they were close. They had to be. The caves were massive here, big enough for giants to pass through. They had to lead out.

'No! This can't be!' Fiona screamed out her frustration. They all stopped, tiredness aching through them. 'What's happening?'

They had reached a wall of stone. Liam ran up to it, and beat his fists against it. 'This can't be!'

Axel ran too, feeling around the stone as if he might

find a lever, and the wall might fly open like Aladdin's cave.

Zesh looked around, flashing his light around the cave. 'There were no other caves leading out, were there?' Had they missed something? Would they have to go back? No! 'There has to be another tunnel here!'

'Well, there's no'!' Fiona screamed. 'No zonking way out.'

She threw herself on the ground, buried her face in her hands. 'They're never going to find us. We'll be here for ever. We'll turn into a bunch of cannibals.'

Axel was folding his fists open and shut angrily. 'I'm no' staying here. If there's a way out I'm gonny find it.'

He was beginning to panic, terrified that the only other way out might be yet another tiny cramped space. And he wouldn't go there again. So, he'd never get out.

'We'll go back. We must have missed something.'

'We can't go back. It's flooded back there.' Liam leaned against the stone. He'd been sure too, expecting at every turning to see light, stretching way ahead of them. He had almost been able to smell the sea. Had they taken a wrong turning? Had they missed another entrance, the right cave? Or was the way out behind them, flooded for another age, and they were indeed trapped in here for ever?

Liam made a sudden mad rush at the prone body of the teacher, flung himself down beside him, grabbed him by the collar. 'Where's the way out!' he shook him. 'How do we find it!'

No one stopped him. Everyone was too tired. Too scared.

Mr Marks stirred once again. His eyelids flickered for a moment, as they had so many times before, but there was no other response.

'So, what do we do now?' Fiona asked. No one answered her. No one knew. 'We're done for this time, ain't we?' She could have cried, but what was the point? 'Done for,' she said again.

'What was that noise?' Fiona was alert. 'I heard a noise there.'

Axel barked at her. 'That's all we do in this place, hear noises.'

But they were all silent, listening.

Then they all heard it, somewhere winding through the caves, reaching them eerily. No mistaking.

'Was that a whistle?' Fiona jumped to her feet, peering into the darkness. 'That was a whistle,' she decided.

They were all on their feet. 'They've found us!' They cried out. 'We're here! Help us!'

'Where's it coming from?'

But it was hard to tell here in the underground.

'Whistle back!' Zesh said, and with that he blew his whistle as loudly as his breath allowed.

The whistle came back in answer, faintly, but moving towards them. Then they all blew, frantically, blowing and shouting and yelling, 'We're here!'

They were jumping and hugging each other, and laughing. 'We're saved!'

One minute, despair, all hope gone. The next, joy. They were saved.

'I knew search parties would be out looking for us,' Zesh said, his confidence returning. 'We probably weren't in any real danger of never being found.'

'Your brain's missing, pal, if you think that.' Fiona sounded angry. 'Angie was certainly in danger, wasn't she?'

'I'm sorry,' Zesh said at once, realising what a stupid thing he had just said.

Fiona laughed then, a relieved laugh, because she was saved. 'Are you listening to this, boys!' she called to Axel and Liam. 'Zesh actually apologised to me, and it's not for the first time.'

She took a deep breath and blew her whistle again.

Louder now, the answering whistle came. 'There!' Liam said, pointing to the wall of rock. 'It's coming from there.'

They all moved closer to the sound. Axel shone his light up and down, he felt all around it. A wall of rock.

'I can still hear that whistle,' Fiona called out. 'Here!'

Suddenly, illuminated by the light from their lamps, a face appeared through the rock. White, ghostly, unreal. And this time when Fiona screamed, it was in terror.

The face was Angie's.

CHAPTER 30

Angie? It couldn't be. Axel stepped back, almost as frightened as he'd been when he'd been stuck fast in the tunnel. Angie was dead. She even looked dead, her face as white as a ghost, her eyes just black pinpoints caught in their lamplights. For a shocked moment no one said a word. Angie looked around them from one to the other.

'Why are you all looking at me like that? It's Angie. Don't you recognise me?'

She began clambering out of the rock. Why hadn't they seen this opening before? That bothered Axel too. They'd searched all around here and found nothing, and suddenly Angie appears, from solid rock, from a cave that hadn't been there before.

'We thought you were dead,' Fiona stuttered the words out. 'I tried to find you. Honest.'

Angie beamed a smile. 'I know you did. I heard you. I tried to let you know where I was, but I had no breath to use my whistle.'

Fiona took her by the shoulders and shook her. 'So why didn't you shout? I was screaming. You could at least have yelled back.'

'I tried, Fiona. You couldn't hear me. I was so scared.'

'We waited for you. I kept listening.' Fiona sounded angry. Anger verging on tears. Relieved Angie was back, just not sure she was actually alive.

'I was trying to come back, but the water started rising. I couldn't find the right way. I had to move on.'

'But where did you go?' Zesh asked her.

Angie smiled at him. 'You got your inhaler back.' She turned to Axel. 'I knew you'd give it to him.'

Axel waited for someone – Liam – to tell her different. But no one did.

'I didn't know where I was going. I was so afraid. But,' she touched Fiona's arm, 'then I remembered what you told me. Remember?'

I told her she was an ugly fat bird, was all Fiona could remember ... that helped her?

'You said, no use moaning, you play the cards you're dealt with. So I thought, right, I'm on my own. That's the cards I've been dealt with, so get on with it. You helped me so much.'

Fiona looked at her in disbelief.

'Anyway, I've found the way out. And we have to go now!'

'You!' Liam was shocked. So was Axel. Fat Angie, the one who screamed her way out of the bat cave, the first one to die … (But of course, she hadn't died, had she?) She was the one who was going to lead them to safety?

'I found signs. Someone must have marked the way a long time ago. One of those legends we heard about, must have been true, I suppose.'

'But how did you find us?'

'Sounds carry in these caves. Have you noticed that? You can actually imagine them winding their way through all the chambers looking for someone to hear them.'

'Angie's back right enough,' Fiona said. 'Doing her zonking creative writing.'

'Sorry,' Angie said softly.

'So you'll be able to find the way back?'

'Sure I will.' No hesitation. 'I've laid signs too. Maybe in years to come, decades, someone will find my signs too.'

Fiona turned to them. 'We forgot, she's a Girl Guide. She's probably got a badge for "Finding your way out of caves".'

Angie smiled. 'I have now,' she said. Then she sighed. 'I missed you guys.'

Axel winced. She missed us guys! That girl would never change.

'Well, are you ready to go? I really think we should hurry.'

'Why?' Fiona asked her.

Angie didn't answer for a moment. She looked around the cave, thinking of an answer, Fiona was sure of it. 'Just believe me. We have to hurry.'

Liam whispered to Axel. 'We're following a dead girl out of a cave. Or is she leading us to our death as well?'

Axel tugged at his sleeve. 'You don't really think she's dead, do you?' He looked at Angie, white-faced, smiling, and he wasn't sure.

*   *   *

We will die of hunger in here. Have other people died of hunger in these black holes? Nothing to eat, nothing can grow. Life needs light. No wonder Hell is in the underworld. And this is Hell.

Yet, it seems different now. There is a heat here. It saps my strength, feels even more claustrophobic. This cave oozes with moisture, and there is so little air that my breath is coming in gasps.

'Surely we must have come the wrong way, sir? Surely we should have found something by now?'

The Captain is looking all around as if he is puzzled too. I see the hesitation in his eyes.

Oh, please, God, let him want to go back. Give him some common sense. I have a feeling of doom in this black hole of Hell.

'Maybe … we have taken a wrong turning.' He turns to me. 'We will go back.'

I promise myself that when I see my first sign I will run, leave him if I have to. I will go no further. I am almost crying with relief as he stumbles towards me, making me throw my hands against the wall to stop myself from falling too.

And the wall is wet.

And the wall is soft.

I hold out my hands as the sticky liquid clings to it.

The wall is soft.

But rock is not soft.

Rock is never soft.

'What is it, boy!' the Captain demands, and I hold out my hands to him

'The wall is soft,' I say.

He looks at me, and then he touches the wall too. I hear his low moan.

The wall is soft.

Rock is not soft. So this cannot be rock. It cannot be wall.

When did the nightmare realisation dawn on me? In what instant?

I do not know.

I looked all around the cave and I screamed.

'We are inside the Worm!'

* * *

Mr Marks stirred uneasily as they lifted him. They stopped and watched him for a moment. Was he going to wake up this time? Angie came towards him and felt his brow.

'I've been giving him water,' Fiona told her. Her tone surprised Zesh. It was as if she wanted to please Angie, to assure her she had taken over her job.

Angie smiled again. 'I knew you would,' she said. Then she turned to them all. 'This way,' and she stepped forwards and disappeared into the black hole.

'I can't believe she's back, Zesh,' Fiona whispered. 'Can you?'

It seemed that none of them could. No wonder they all seemed scared of her. She had gone, disappeared, and now, she had reappeared just like magic. It gave Zesh a chill feeling in his stomach. 'But she knows the way out,' he said. 'What choice do we have but to follow her?'

Liam said softly. 'Well, I'm telling you this. I'm keeping my eye on her. I don't trust her.'

Axel tried to make a joke of it. 'Liam thinks she's the evil ghost of Angie, come back to lead us to our deaths.' No one laughed.

Liam didn't even dispute it. 'I'm gonny watch her anyway.'

They moved into the tunnel, and it seemed to Zesh that they were going the wrong way, going back, going down. He glanced at Axel. Axel whose sense of direction was always good. And saw concern on his face too. Axel felt him watching him. 'Where is she taking us?'

Angie caught the whispered words. 'It leads to the sea. Honest.' Her eyes went wide. 'Look. There's one of my signs.'

Her sign was a pile of rocks built into a pyramid. 'This is the way I came.'

Axel and Zesh stared at each other. What choice did they have indeed, but to follow her?

As they struggled deeper the water began to run down the cave walls and the smell grew musty.

None of them liked it.

'I don't think this is right!' Liam yelled.

Angie's voice was calm when she answered him. 'Wait till you see the signs.'

'What signs!' Liam yelled again. 'What are you talking about?'

'Signs, numbers. I found them, like a countdown to the sea. 10, 9, 8. Come on.' She seemed to glance behind her, and her smile wavered.

They all felt it. Something ominous in the dark.

'Please. Hurry,' Angie said.

'Do you think there's going to be another collapse?' Liam asked Zesh.

But a collapse was the last thing on Zesh's mind.

Not one of them felt easy about following Angie, but at least they were moving. And if Zesh thought the caves were growing darker, he refused to be afraid. If this was the way that would lead them out, that was all that mattered.

But what if it didn't?

Liam had put it into their heads that Angie might be … no, that was stupid. He was letting his imagination take over. It was the dark. In the dark anything was possible.

*   *   *

My scream and his send tremors that disturb it. I feel it move under my feet.

We are inside the Worm!

No wonder the stench, the oppressive heat.

We are in the belly of the Worm.

We begin to run. In front of me I can see the open mouth of the cave.

No. Not the cave, I see that now. The mouth of the Worm.

Wide and open.

Our only escape, that way.

We are both running for our lives. Screaming in terror. I slip on the slime beneath my feet, and the Captain runs past me.

'Captain!' I try to stand but I keep slipping. 'Captain, do not leave me!'

I must not be left in here, to be digested slowly by the Worm.

He does not stop. He will leave me and save himself.

That terror alone gets me up and steady and I begin running again.

And as I run I realise that the mouth is closing slowly. Closing, trapping us inside.

No!

Like an athlete I run. Like an Olympic athlete I run. No one should die this way.

I am beside the Captain now. He is struggling, his face strained with terror.

I pass him. The mouth is closing. I must get out. I must throw myself the last few feet. Hurl myself forwards and outside of the mouth.

I am free. Free.

I turn and urge the Captain on. And still that mouth is closing … closing.

He is screaming so loud my ears bleed with the pain.

RUN!

But he will not make it. He knows it. He screams to me. 'Don't leave me here!'

But what am I to do?

Nothing.

Nothing but watch as the mouth closes on his terrified face.

* * *

Axel was afraid too. Afraid of Angie. Why was he following her, listening to her? Especially after what Liam had put into his head. But he wanted desperately to be out of here. To wide open space. He wanted to see the sky. Breathe air. He breathed in and the smell was putrid. There was a sound, like someone, something, letting its breath out. Behind him.

He began to hurry.

* * *

I cannot rest. For I see the thing begin to move, sliding towards me. It is as if the whole cave is moving. It is coming after me.

No!

* * *

I'm off my chump, Fiona was thinking. I'm shaking like a leaf and I'm beginning to run as if there was something after me. Or maybe the something's here. She looked ahead at Angie, half hidden in the gloom. Angie turned right at that instant and smiled at her. Fiona shivered. Why was she so afraid? More afraid than she'd been since they had come down here? The caves seemed to be whispering to her. Zonks! She was beginning to sound like Angie.

'Look, Fiona!' Angie was pointing to another sign, a number on the rocks. 9 scraped in stone. 'This way.'

Was that the gushing of water she could hear behind her, above her, around her? 'Are you sure, Angie?'

Angie hurried ahead. 'I'm sure.'

* * *

I look desperately for my signs. The numbers I scratched so hurriedly as I stumbled behind the Captain. The Captain! I try not to think of his fate. I will go mad if I do. I am almost mad already. It is behind me, like a rush of water, like the tide.

At last, my sign. 8. I run on.

*   *   *

Liam had a bad feeling about all this. To him, Angie didn't seem real. How could she have survived on her own, found her way out, and come back to them? And why would she do it? She could have organised a rescue party to come for them. Better able to find them, to help them than she was. No. Something wasn't right about all this. And now, they seemed in even more danger than they'd ever been.

She turned and looked right at him, almost as if she could read his thoughts. 'We have to hurry,' she said.

There was a sudden sigh through the caves. A sigh that seemed to be moving closer. Angie heard it too and caught her breath. She urged them on faster. 'Look, we're almost there!' Her light shone on another number. *7*. Written as if by a foreign hand.

'Come on! Let's go!'

It was coming behind them, that long sigh, as if

273

something giant and dark, filling the cave, was coming after them.

*　*　*

I dare not look behind me, though I can almost feel its putrid breath against my back. It must not get me. My screams are mixed with the sound of it, the almost silent sound of it oozing behind me.

I am almost there. 6.

*　*　*

They all began to run, hauling the teacher between them, hardly daring to glance behind them.

Whatever was behind them was coming ever closer, oozing through the chambers, filling them with terror.

They screamed. They yelled. They ran. And still it came behind them.

*　*　*

If I stumble once it will catch me and it must not catch me. I turn my head. I must see how close it is …

Ah! It is too close, and its mouth is beginning to slowly open again … for me.

*　*　*

The light. At last, Fiona saw the light. She had thought she would never see it again – and there it was, just a pinpoint in the darkness, but it was light.

It gave her the strength to run faster, to try to forget whatever horror was there behind them.

She risked a glance at Zesh. His mouth was open wide as if he was gasping for breath. He looked at her too and she knew from his eyes that he had seen the light too.

He hadn't the breath to speak, so she spoke for him, calling out to the rest. 'Daylight! Look!'

It looked as if Axel grew in height. Fiona could feel his power as he lifted Mr Marks higher, practically taking all his weight. Liam, skinny little Liam, was hauling him with the rest, as they saw the light coming closer.

Fiona prayed. Her mind a jumble of thoughts all coming together at once. What if it's not daylight! What if Angie really is a ghost, and we're dead too and don't know it, and she's come back for us, to lead us into the light! She'd seen that in a film once. That's what they do, dead people, they head for the light.

And behind them, was a devil from Hell trying to keep them here?

Nightmare thoughts, running round her head, and no time to work them out. Just keep going. No matter what was ahead, it had to be better than what was behind them.

* * *

It's getting closer, Axel was thinking. Whatever's behind us is getting closer and I am frightened. I don't want to know what it is, I don't dare look behind me. Why wasn't he dropping the teacher? He could run faster without him, yet something was stopping him, he didn't know what.

He saw the light too, felt a cool breath against his face. Was that the touch of Death?

Stop thinking like that!

Run!

Liam was afraid to look back. He felt the cold breath too, making the hairs on his neck stand on end. And the stench of something too. Something long dead.

Get out of here! he was screaming inside. Get out of here before it catches us!

* * *

Get out of here! I am screaming inside. Get out of here before it catches me!

CHAPTER 31

The cave opened like a mouth, spitting them out one by one. They threw themselves screaming with joy and relief against the rocks of the Doon.

Zesh was the first to look back into that black cave. Did he see something? Something disappointed, oozing back into the darkness, winding itself down tunnels and chasms and chambers to its lair?

'It's nothing. It was our imagination,' Liam said to him, following his eyes, knowing what he was thinking.

Zesh grabbed for his inhaler and sucked into it before he said a word. 'Something was after us. I was sure of it.'

Axel was breathless. 'What are you trying to say it was? That Worm? Don't talk daft. There's no such thing.' But his voice was shaking.

'Of course there isn't,' Zesh agreed. 'Of course there isn't.'

Fiona stood up and stretched. Her fears all behind her. Here in the open air, with clouds scuttling across the blue sky and gulls squawking, she was afraid of nothing again. She looked at Angie, sitting solid as rock beside her. Why had she been so afraid? Angie was as alive as she was, and she was alive too!

'Stupid the way your imagination can play tricks on you,' she said aloud without realising it. 'Especially in the dark.'

'If it *was* our imagination,' Zesh said.

Axel splashed his face with water. 'Of course it was. There is no such thing as the Worm!'

'But there is.'

It was Angie who said it, sitting on the rocks, the foam from the waves splashing against her legs. They gaped at her.

'Why do you think I came back for you, and didn't go for a search party? I saw it. There in one of the tunnels. Waiting for you.'

'Get real,' Axel said. 'Don't believe you.'

'But it's true. I saw it.' She covered her face with her hands. 'It was horrible, horrible. It's not just a legend. It really exists. The Worm.'

Liam tried to laugh. He didn't convince anyone. He

looked back into the cave, into that blackness. He was remembering how scared he had been just moments ago. 'No. It was your imagination, Angie.' He wanted to convince himself as well as her.

She shook her head and her lip trembled. 'But you didn't see it. I did.'

Axel said. 'And it didn't eat you?'

She shook her head and stared him out. ' It was waiting, waiting there in the cave. Waiting for you.'

'Aye, right,' he said. That couldn't be true. She must be lying, he was thinking.

No one believed her. No one wanted to believe her. Not here in the open air, with the spray from the sea on their faces. There was no Worm. There couldn't be.

No one spoke for a long time. It had all been in their imagination. It had all been in Angie's.

Fiona shielded her eyes and looked up at the sky. 'Right! Where's this zonking search party!'

'Well, now I've seen everything,' Rick said, looking across the school cafeteria. 'It looks as if Marks is actually smiling at Axel.'

It didn't surprise Zesh. Not now, not after what they had all come through – underworld.

'He did thank him, publicly, from the platform of the school assembly hall,' Zesh reminded his friend. In fact, the teacher had thanked them all. Without them, he would certainly have died.

'Yeah, another miracle.' Rick laughed. 'And who would have thought that me not being picked for that trip would be a blessing in disguise?'

'Yeah, you did all right. You got to go to Paris instead.'

Rick got to Paris! Zesh hadn't known till he came back that someone had had to cancel and Rick had got their place.

'No. I don't mean just that, but look what happened to you! Trapped under there, with that lot. Your worst nightmare.'

Zesh said nothing. There was a lot they hadn't told about what had happened. An unspoken oath between them to keep so much to themselves. No one knew Axel had taken his inhaler. No one knew Axel had been trapped in stone, and panicked. No one knew that Axel and Liam had gone on by themselves. No one knew that Zesh had been willing to leave the teacher behind.

Their secrets.

Their story had only been a minor item in a local paper, on the regional news. A helicopter had been sent out, and cave rescue had been alerted. Somewhere, inside the caves, another search party had been looking for them. But not for long enough for them to become a national sensation.

Yet, they could all have sworn they had been trapped for days on end.

Axel brushed past him just then. 'Hi, Zesh, seen Liam?'

Zesh stretched his neck and spotted Liam chatting at the cafeteria door. 'Over there, Axel. How's things?'

'Great, Zesh. See ya!'

Zesh watched him bound across to Liam and put a friendly arm on his shoulder. They laughed together at some joke. Why had he never noticed how much taller than Axel Liam was? It was clear the two boys were friends. Not the way they had been before, but real friends.

And Zesh and Axel? They would never be friends, but they'd never be enemies again.

Rick was watching them too. 'I suppose it stands to reason. Trapped down there, together. Having to rely on each other. I suppose it changes things.'

'You talk such a load of baloney, Rick!' It was Fiona coming behind them. 'What do you think we were doing down there ... bonding?' She gave Zesh a dunt that sent him hurtling against a wall. 'Did he tell you he owes his life to me! Did he tell you that!'

She let out one of her belly laughs. She really did not laugh like a girl at all!

'Thanks to me she's stopped smoking,' Zesh said smugly.

'I know, but it's a drastic way to stop. Now, I'm tryin' to get my mother off them as well.'

Zesh studied her for a moment. 'You know, I've been thinking, Fiona ...'

'Well, there's a first time for everything.' Fiona had to get that in.

'I could teach you to speak good English. I could make a lady out of you.'

Fiona laughed for ages. 'What, you mean ... you Professor Higgins, me Eliza Dolittle? I don't think.'

Zesh fell back in a mock swoon. 'You have read *Pygmalion*?'

'Pig ... what? It's *My Fair Lady*, thicko! Do you know nothing? It was on the telly last week.'

And when he roared with laughter at that, she knew

that Zesh would always get on her wick!

And the Worm?

No one would ever believe such an outrageous story. And they all decided, without having to discuss it, that none of them had really seen it anyway.

It was a legend. A story told in the dark, to make you afraid. The dark can play strange tricks on your imagination. Make you see things that aren't really there.

And when your imagination takes over anything can happen.

They didn't want to be laughed at.

The only one of them who talked about it was Angie. And no one believed her. She was mocked and made a fool of. They discovered she had a history of telling tall tales, of making up stories.

She had seen the Worm? That was like saying she had seen the Loch Ness Monster. Unbelievable.

And Angie was gone now, moved once again, to another school, another story.

'I still say she was dead,' Liam would say. Nothing would ever convince him otherwise.

And though they never talked of it, sometimes Zesh would catch a look from one of them when they passed each other in the corridor. A look that seemed to say ...

'It *was* only our imagination ... a legend ... wasn't it?'

I am an old man now. If I write my story, who would believe me? And do I believe it now myself? It is only an old legend. A story told around the camp fires on a dark night.

So long ago.

Yet, I will never forget the terrified eyes of my Captain as the mouth of the Worm closed on him.

Cathy MACPHAIL
Run Zan Run

Cathy MACPHAIL
Missing

Cathy MACPHAIL
Bad Company

Cathy MACPHAIL
Dark Waters

Cathy MACPHAIL
Fighting Back

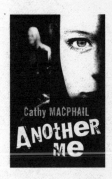

Cathy MACPHAIL
Another Me

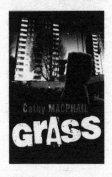

Cathy MACPHAIL
Grass

Cathy MACPHAIL
Roxy's Baby

Cathy MACPHAIL
Worse than Boys

'YOUNG FICTION IS GOING FROM STRENGTH TO STRENGTH, LED BY AUTHORS LIKE CATHY MACPHAIL.' *THE BOOKSELLER*